Go ahead and scream.

No one can hear you. You're no longer in the safe world you know.

You've taken a terrifying step . . .

into the darkest corners of your imagination.

You've opened the door to . . .

the NIGHTMARE room

the NIGHTMARE room

My Name Is Evil

R.L. STINE

AVON BOOKS
An Imprint of HarperCollinsPublishers

PARACHUTE PRESS

My Name Is Evil

For information address:
HarperCollins Children's Books,
a Divison of HarperCollins Publishers,
1350 Avenue of the Americas,
New York, NY 10019.

Library of Congress Catalog Card Number: 00-190245
ISBN 0-06-440901-5

First Avon edition, 2000

Visit us on the World Wide Web!
www.harperchildrens.com

Welcome...

I'm R.L. Stine. Let me introduce you to Maggie O'Connor. She's the red-haired girl with the excited smile on her face.

Why is she smiling? Well, today is Maggie's birthday. She's thirteen today—and what could be better than celebrating this special time with her three best friends?

They've taken Maggie to the little carnival on the pier. And now they've stopped outside the fortune-teller's tent. "Let's go in," one of Maggie's friends urges. "You have to have your fortune told on your birthday!"

Maggie follows her friends inside. The fortune-teller picks up Maggie's hand and starts to read her palm. . . .

In a few seconds, the tent will ring out with Maggie's cries of horror.

Happy birthday, Maggie. But be careful. When you step into the fortune-teller's tent, you're stepping into . . . *THE NIGHTMARE ROOM*.

"Maggie, you're so evil!" Jackie Mullen said, laughing.

My mouth dropped open. "Huh? Me? Evil?"

Jackie pointed across the table to the cupcakes on my plate. "You took three cupcakes and only ate the icing."

Her sister Judy frowned at me. "What's wrong with them? I baked them myself—for your birthday."

I licked chocolate icing off my fingers. "There's nothing wrong with them," I told her. "They're wicked cool cupcakes. I just like icing."

Jackie laughed again. "Are you getting weird? You never say wicked cool."

I sneered at her. "I'm thirteen now. I can say whatever I want. Besides, I need a new image."

"Like a makeover," Judy said.

"Like a personality makeover," Jilly, the third sister said. "Maggie wants to be sophisticated now."

Jilly was right about that. I've always been the youngest in my class because I skipped second grade. But now I was turning thirteen. Now I was old enough to transform myself into a mature, confident person. And no one would treat me like "the baby" anymore.

"I am sophisticated," I said. "I'm thirteen now, and there's no turning back!"

"Well, you're off to a bad start," Jackie said. She pointed. "You have icing in your hair."

I groaned and reached up and felt sticky stuff up there. For some reason, the three sisters all thought it was a riot. Jilly laughed so hard, she choked on her cupcake.

Jackie, Judy, and Jilly Mullen are triplets, which means that I have three best friends. Everyone at our school—Cedar Bay Middle School—calls them the Three J's. And they're very close, although they try really hard to be different from each other.

Jackie and Judy look alike. They both have straight black hair and big, round brown eyes. They both always look as if they're suntanned.

But they're so eager for people to tell them apart, they have totally different styles. Jackie's hair is long, halfway down her back. She wears funky, old clothes, baggy jeans, old bell-bottoms from the seventies, oversized, bright-colored tops she finds at garage sales. She loves clanky jewelry, heavy beads, and dangling, plastic earrings.

Judy is much more preppy. She has her hair cut very short. She wears short skirts over black tights and neat little vests. Judy always looks as if she just washed her face.

Jilly was born last, and she doesn't look as if she belongs in the same family. She has long, golden blond hair, creamy, pale skin, and big green eyes. She looks very angelic, and she talks in a soft, whispery voice.

Jackie is funny, and kind of loud, and a real joker. She doesn't take things too seriously. I really want to be like that.

I have coppery hair and a slender, serious face. I've been quiet and pretty shy and serious my whole life. And I keep thinking if I hang out with Jackie a lot, maybe I'll be more like her.

Judy is the brain in the group. She is the perfect student. It's all I can do just to keep up in school. But Judy is always busy writing essays and doing projects for extra credit.

Judy likes to organize things. She's always joining clubs and committees at school. These days, she is organizing a huge Pet Fair to raise money for animal rights.

And Jilly? Well . . . as my mother would say, Jilly is in her own world. In other words, she's kind of a flake. She's really into boys, and music, and I-don't-know-what-else. She's kind of a dreamy person. You know. Like she's floating a few feet off the ground.

The only thing I've ever seen Jilly be serious about is her dancing. She takes ballet lessons five times a week after school, and she's really talented.

I'm into dance, too. But I've always been too shy to try out for anything. Not anymore, though. In a few days, the "new" me and Jilly are both trying out for a community ballet company. My whole life I've dreamed of dancing with a real company, but I'm not looking forward to the audition—because I have to compete against Jilly!

Anyway, those are my best friends, the Three J's. And of course I wanted to spend my thirteenth birthday at their house with them.

When we finished the birthday cupcakes and I wiped the chocolate icing from my hair, Jackie jumped up, clapped her hands once, and said, "Let's go!"

"Go where?" I asked.

"You'll see," Judy said. She started to pull me from the table. "Just follow us."

"To the carnival," Jilly added, tying her blond hair back with a blue, ribbony scrunchie.

I held back. "Huh? The carnival on the pier?"

All three girls nodded. All three were grinning. They had planned this.

So I didn't argue. I followed them to the carnival. And that's when all the horror began.

A short while later the four of us staggered off the roller coaster, laughing, holding on to each other to keep from falling over. I blinked, trying to stop the ground from tilting and swaying. The carnival lights flashed in my eyes.

"That was awesome!" Jilly declared, brushing back her blond curls with both hands.

I held my stomach. "Wow. I'm so glad I ate all those cupcakes!"

"Why do they call it the Blue Beast?" Judy asked. "The cars are bright yellow!"

Good question. Judy always wanted things to make sense.

"Who would want to ride on the Yellow Beast?" Jackie asked.

We all thought that was a riot, and we laughed our heads off as we made our way across the pier.

It was a warm, cloudy night. The air felt heavy and damp, more like summer than fall. I glanced up, looking for the moon. But the low clouds blocked it out.

"Wasn't this a great idea?" Jackie asked, taking my arm. Judy hurried up ahead to buy more ride tickets. "Isn't this the perfect way to celebrate?"

"Wicked cool," I replied, grinning.

Jackie shook her fist at me. "Go ahead, Maggie. Say it again. I dare you."

"I think there are some boys from school here," Jilly said. She has the most amazing Boy Radar! "Maybe I'll catch you guys later."

She started to wander off, but Judy pulled her back. "Let's stick together for a while, Jilly. It's a party, remember?"

The carnival opens on the pier every summer. It's kind of tacky, but we hang out there sometimes on weekend nights. There isn't much else to do in Cedar Bay.

Fall had arrived. In a week or two they'd be shutting the carnival down and packing up. Some of the rides were already closed. And the big Fun House sign lay on its side on the ground, the paint chipped and fading.

We wandered through a long row of game booths. "Try your luck, girls!" a man shouted, holding up three baseballs. "You can't lose! Really!"

I stopped across from a brightly lit booth. A young woman stood in front of a wall of balloons. "Hey—darts. Want to throw some darts? I'm pretty good at that."

Jackie shook her head. "No way. Let's do something wild."

I squinted at her. "Something wild?"

"Yeah. Something really crazy," Jilly chimed in, her green eyes flashing. "Something we normally wouldn't do. For your birthday."

"But darts is fun," Judy argued. "If Maggie wants to throw darts . . ."

That's why I like Judy. She's always on my side.

"Forget darts," Jackie said, pulling me across the row of booths. "I see the perfect thing. Awesome!"

She dragged me to the door of a low, square building. I gasped when I read the red-and-black hand-lettered sign next to the door: TATTOOS WHILE-U-WAIT.

"Whoa! No way!" I cried. I tried to pull back. But Jackie was too strong. She tugged me through the doorway.

The little room was dark and hot, and smelled of incense and tobacco. Red and blue tattoo samples on jagged pieces of paper were tacked up and down the walls.

Jackie hadn't let go of my arm. "Check them out. I'll buy you one for your birthday!" she said.

I stared at her. "You're kidding—right?"

"Ooh, look at this one!" Jilly gushed. She pointed to a blue half-moon circled by red stars. "That's the prettiest one. Or how about this red flower?"

"Doesn't it hurt to get tattooed?" Judy asked Jackie.

Jackie picked up a long needle from a workbench

7

against the wall. She pressed the tip against the back of my hand. "Zip zip zip, and it's done," she said. "Can you imagine the look on your mother's face when you come home with a tattoo?"

"No way!" I cried. "Come on—I don't want any tattoo!"

I tried to pull free of Jackie's grasp. And as I did, a large tattoo tacked up beside the door caught my eye.

It was so ugly. A dragon's head. A snarling green dragon with its jaws open, red flames bursting from its gaping nostrils. And beneath it, red words with blue shadows behind them. Bold, bloodred words:

My Name Is EVIL!

As I stared at the ugly tattoo, I felt a chill run down my back. It seemed to hypnotize me or something. I couldn't turn away from it. Couldn't take my eyes off it.

Finally Jackie's voice cut through the spell. "Pick one. Hurry."

"N-no," I whispered. "Let's get out of here!"

I headed for the door, but Jackie gripped my arm from behind. "Grab her," she ordered the others. "Don't let her get away!"

They held on to me tightly, staring at me in cold silence.

Jackie broke up first. "Wow! I think you really believed us!"

Jilly laughed too. "You did! You thought we were serious."

Judy frowned. "Maggie, I told them it was a mean joke. But they wouldn't listen to me."

I stared angrily at Jackie. "You—you creep! You really scared me," I confessed. "How could you do that?"

Jackie laughed. "Easy!"

"Jackie has a sick sense of humor," Judy said, still frowning.

"Ha ha," I said, rolling my eyes.

Jackie shrugged. She put her arm around my shoulders. "I'm sorry, Maggie. I really didn't think you'd believe us."

I sighed. "I always fall for dumb jokes. Not too sophisticated, huh?"

"Forget about it," Jilly said. "Now you're thirteen, remember? Makeover time?"

I sighed again. I felt really dumb.

Why did I think that my best friends in the world would force me to do something I didn't want to do?

Why did I panic like that?

The four of us stumbled out into the warm night. Across the path a tall girl was heaving baseballs at a target, trying to dunk a young man in a swim tank.

A mother hurried past, pulling two little boys. Both boys carried huge cones of pink cotton candy. They had the stuff stuck all over their cheeks and noses.

"Let's have some fun!" Jackie declared. She still had her arm around my shoulder. The four of us walked side by side in a solid row.

Jackie pulled back when she saw Glen Martin. I saw him, too. He was with two other guys from school. They were all singing some kind of song, snapping their fingers as they walked, bopping along.

"Oh, wow," Jackie muttered.

I glanced at her. What did she mean by that?

Everyone in school knows that I have a crush on Glen. Everyone except Glen, that is.

I watched him come nearer. He is tall and lanky, and he's so cute with his wild, curly brown hair, which he never brushes, and serious dark eyes.

Glen is always goofing, always cracking jokes. He's always in trouble in school for breaking up the class. He has the greatest laugh. And when he smiles, two cute dimples appear on his cheeks.

Glen doesn't live in my neighborhood. He lives in a tiny house in the old part of town. And the guys he hangs out with are kind of tough.

Sometimes I think about inviting Glen over or something. But I always lose my nerve.

That's going to change, too. It's makeover time, I reminded myself. And I'm going to invite Glen over real soon.

"Hey—it's the Three J's!" one of Glen's friends called.

"Yeah. Jokey, Jumpy, and Jerk-Face," Glen said.

Jackie tossed back her hair and sneered at him. "That's a compliment, coming from you—Tarzan!"

That's so mean, I thought. I can't believe Jackie is still calling him Tarzan! The name made Glen blush.

"Hey, guys. What's up?" Jilly walked over to Glen's two friends and started flirting with them.

Judy sighed impatiently. "Are we just going to stand here? Aren't we going to do any rides?"

Glen grinned at Jackie. "You'd better hurry. The Ugly Dog Contest is starting over there." He pointed to a tent at the end of the pier. "You could win a dog bone!"

Jackie scowled at him. "Shut up, Glen."

His dark eyes flashed. "You shut up." He grabbed the beaded necklace Jackie always wears and gave it a tug.

"Let go!" she screamed.

I stepped between them. "Come on—be nice," I said. "It's my birthday."

Glen turned to me and his eyes flashed, as if seeing me for the first time. "Maggie—hey. Is it really your birthday?"

I nodded. "Yeah. We all came here to celebrate, and—"

"Wow! It was my birthday yesterday!" he declared.

Before I could utter a reply, he grabbed my hand and shook it. "Happy birthday to us!" he cried.

And then, believe it or not, he raised my hand to his mouth—and planted a wet, noisy, slobbery kiss on the back of it.

His friends laughed. Judy and Jilly laughed, too.

I stood there stunned.

Glen started to back away.

Then Jackie shoved me from behind—shoved me into Glen. "Go ahead—kiss your boyfriend!" she cried.

Glen and I stumbled over each other and nearly tumbled to the ground. Everyone laughed. They thought it was a riot.

"Jackie—give me a break!" I shouted angrily. How could she embarrass me like that?

Glen backed away, blushing again. "Happy birthday. Catch you later." He flashed me a thumbs-up and started off with his friends.

A few seconds later the Three J's and I were hurrying away, heading past the Tilt-A-Whirl and FreeFall Mountain. Shrill screams rose up all around us.

Judy and Jilly were giggling about something. Jackie twined her arm around mine and pulled me along. "He is such a geek!" she exclaimed. "How can you like him?"

"He totally hates us!" Jilly declared.

"Especially Jackie," Judy added.

"And I don't blame him," I said. "Jackie depantsed him in front of the whole school!"

Jackie laughed. "What an awesome moment!"

"It almost caused a riot!" Jilly said. "Poor Glen was embarrassed for life!"

Judy sighed. "Another one of Jackie's great jokes."

"I can't believe you're still calling him Tarzan," I said. "That was a whole year ago."

Last year Jackie was in charge of costumes for the talent show at school. And Glen decided to do a crazy comedy act wearing a Tarzan costume. Well, Jackie had this insane idea. Somehow she rigged Glen's costume. She secretly removed most of the elastic.

And there was poor Glen, onstage in front of the entire school. And Jackie's trick worked. His pants dropped to his ankles in front of everyone!

"I'll never forget those black bikini briefs he was wearing!" Jackie exclaimed. All three sisters exploded with laughter.

"He looked like such a geek!" Jilly cried. "Standing there onstage in the stupid black underpants, trying to cover himself up."

"He just stood there. He froze," Jackie remembered. "And the whole auditorium went wild. Everyone just freaked."

"We've called him Tarzan ever since," Jilly said. "It makes him blush every time."

"It was a year ago. You should let it drop. Give him a break," I said.

"Why? Because he's your boyfriend?" Jackie teased.

"It was so mean! Why did you do it in the first place?" I asked.

She fiddled with the tiny glass beads on her necklace and grinned. "I don't know. I just thought it would be funny."

"Hey, check it out. A fortune-teller!" Jilly said. She pointed to a small black tent that stood beside an ice-cream cart. "Can we do it? I love fortune-tellers!"

"No way," I said. "They make me nervous. I don't even like watching them in movies."

"Come on, Maggie. It's your birthday," Jackie said, pulling me to the tent. "You have to have your fortune told on your birthday."

"Let's see what the fortune-teller says about you and Glen!" Jilly teased.

"I don't think so," I said.

But as usual, they didn't give me a choice. A few seconds later we were standing at the doorway to the dark tent.

"We'll all have our fortunes told," Jackie said. "My treat."

"This is so cool!" Jilly whispered. "Do you think it's a real psychic? Do you think she can really tell the future?"

The three sisters started into the tent. I held back, staring at the red-and-black hand-lettered sign: MISS ELIZABETH. FORTUNE-TELLER. ONE DOLLAR.

I suddenly realized that my heart was racing.

Why do I feel so weird? I wondered. Why do I have such a bad feeling about this?

I followed my friends into the tent. The air inside felt hot and steamy. Two electric lanterns on the back tent wall splashed gray light over the fortune-teller's small table.

Miss Elizabeth sat hunched with her elbows on the table, head in her hands, staring into a red glass ball. She didn't look up as we stepped inside. I couldn't tell if she was concentrating on the red ball, or if she was asleep.

The tent was completely bare, except for her table and two wooden chairs, and a large black-and-white poster of a human hand. The hand was divided into sections. There was a lot of writing all over the poster, too small for me to read in the smoky, gray light.

As she stared into the red glass ball, the fortune-teller muttered to herself. She was a middle-aged woman, slender, with bony arms poking out from the sleeves of her red dress, and very large, pale white hands. Squinting into the light, I saw that the polish on her long fingernails matched the red of her dress.

"Hel-lo?" Jackie called, breaking the silence.

Miss Elizabeth finally looked up. She was kind of pretty. She had big, round black eyes and dramatic red-lipsticked lips. Her hair was long and wavy, solid black except for a wide white streak down the middle.

Her eyes moved from one of us to the other. She didn't smile. "Walter, we have visitors," she announced in a hoarse, scratchy voice.

I glanced around, searching for Walter.

"Walter is my late husband," the fortune-teller announced. "He helps me channel information from the spirits."

Jackie and I exchanged glances.

"We'd like you to tell our fortunes," Jilly said.

Miss Elizabeth nodded solemnly. "One dollar each." She held out her long, pale hand. "Four dollars please."

Jackie fumbled in her bag and pulled out four crumpled dollar bills. She handed them to the fortune-teller, who shoved them into a pocket of her red dress.

"Who wants to go first?" Again, her eyes moved slowly over our faces.

"I'll go," Jilly volunteered. She dropped into the chair across the table from Miss Elizabeth.

The fortune-teller lowered her head again to gaze into the red ball. "Walter, bring me the words of the spirit world about this young woman."

I suddenly felt a chill at the back of my neck. I knew I shouldn't be frightened. The woman had to be a fake—right? Otherwise, she wouldn't be working in a tacky carnival like this one.

But she was so serious. So solemn. She didn't seem to be putting on an act.

Now she took Jilly's hand. She pulled it up close to her face and began to study Jilly's palm. Muttering to herself, she moved her long finger back and forth, following the lines of the palm, tracing them with her bright red fingernail.

Jackie leaned close to me. "This is cool," she whispered.

Judy sighed. "This is going to take forever."

Jackie raised a finger to her lips and motioned for Judy to shush.

The woman studied Jilly's palm for a long time, squeezing the hand as she gazed at it, murmuring to Walter in the red glass ball. Finally she raised her eyes to Jilly. "You are artistic," she said in her scratchy voice.

"Yes!" Jilly declared.

"You are a . . . dancer," Miss Elizabeth continued. "You study the dance. You are a hard worker."

"Whoa. I don't believe this!" Jilly gushed. "How do you know—?"

"You have much talent," the fortune-teller murmured, ignoring Jilly's question. "Much talent. But sometimes . . . I see . . . your artistic side gets in the way of your practical side. You are . . . you are . . ."

She shut her eyes. "Help me, Walter," she whispered. Then she opened her eyes again and raised them to Jilly's palm. "You are a very social person. Your friends mean a lot to you. Especially . . . boy friends."

Jackie and Judy laughed. Jilly flashed them an angry scowl. "I—I don't believe this," she told the fortune-teller. "You have everything right!"

"It is my gift," Miss Elizabeth replied softly.

"Will I make the new dance company?" Jilly asked her. "Tryouts are next week. Will I be accepted?"

Miss Elizabeth stared into the glass ball. "Walter?" she whispered.

I held my breath, waiting for the answer. Jilly and I were both trying out for the dance company. And I knew there was only room for one of us.

"Walter can find no answer," the fortune-teller told Jilly. "He only groans." She let go of Jilly's hand.

"He—groaned?" Jilly asked. "Why?"

"Your time is up," Miss Elizabeth said. She motioned to us. "Who is next?"

Jackie shoved Judy forward. Judy dropped into the chair and held her hand out to Miss Elizabeth.

Jilly came running over to join Jackie and me at the edge of the tent. "Isn't she amazing?" she whispered.

"Yes, she is," I had to admit. How did she know

so many true things about Jilly? I was beginning to believe Miss Elizabeth really had powers.

And now I didn't feel afraid or nervous. I was eager to see what the fortune-teller would say about me.

She squeezed Judy's hand and gazed deep into Judy's dark eyes. "You have great love in you," she announced. "Great love for . . . animals."

Judy gasped. "Y-yes!"

"You care for them. You work . . ."

"Yes," Judy said. "I work in an animal shelter after school. That's amazing!"

Miss Elizabeth ran a red fingernail down Judy's palm. "You also have an animal that you care about very much. A dog . . . No. A cat."

"Yes. My cat. Plumper."

Judy turned to us, her face filled with astonishment. "Do you believe this? She's right about everything!"

"I know! It's so cool!" Jilly exclaimed. She swept back her blond hair with a toss of her head. She kept bouncing up and down. She seemed too excited to stand still.

The fortune-teller spent a few more minutes with Judy. She told Judy that she would have a long, successful life. She said Judy would have a big family someday.

"Of kids? Of animals?" Judy asked.

Miss Elizabeth didn't answer.

Next came Jackie's turn. Once again Miss Elizabeth

was right on-target with everything she said. "Wow," Jackie kept muttering. "Wow."

Finally I found myself in the chair across from the fortune-teller. Suddenly I felt nervous again. My mouth was dry. My legs were shaking.

Miss Elizabeth looked older from close up. When she smiled at me, the thick makeup on her face cracked. Tiny drops of sweat glistened at her hairline.

"What is your name?" she asked in a whisper.

"Maggie," I told her.

She nodded solemnly and took my hand. She raised my palm close to her face and squinted down at it in the gray light.

I held my breath. And waited. What would she see?

She squeezed my hand. Brought it closer to her face.

And then . . . then . . . her eyes bulged wide. She let out a loud gasp.

With a violent jerk she tossed my hand away.

And jumped to her feet. Her chair fell behind her, clattering to the tent floor.

She stared at me—stared in open-mouthed horror.

And then she screamed:

"Get OUT! Get AWAY from here!!"

"Huh? Wait—" I choked out.

"Get OUT! You bring EVIL! You bring EVIL with you! Get OUT of here!"

I stumbled out of the tent, my heart pounding.

The air felt cool on my face. I sucked in several deep breaths.

My three friends tumbled out after me. Jackie was the only one laughing. Judy and Jilly were shaking their heads.

I started to jog along the path between the rides. I wanted to get as far away from that crazy woman as I could!

Screams from the roller coaster rang in my ears. And over that shrill sound, the fortune-teller's frantic shrieks repeated in my mind.

"Get OUT! You bring EVIL! You bring EVIL with you! Get OUT of here!"

I stopped running and pressed my back against a tall wooden fence at the edge of the pier. The Three J's hurried up to me. "Wh-why did she say that?" I gasped.

Judy and Jilly both shrugged.

"It was . . . crazy!" Judy whispered.

"But why did she say that about me?" I repeated breathlessly.

Jackie laughed and gave me a playful shove. "Because you're a witch!" she cried.

"But—but—" I stammered.

Jackie imitated the fortune-teller's scratchy voice: "You're evil, Maggie. Get out of here! You're so evil, you're scaring Walter!"

Jackie sounded so much like Miss Elizabeth, I had to laugh.

"Let me see your hand." Jackie grabbed my hand and pulled my palm up to her face. "Yuck! You are evil!" she cried. "That's the most evil hand I ever saw!"

They started laughing all over again. But this time I didn't join in.

"She seemed so serious," I said, picturing the whole scene again. "And then when she looked at my hand, she really did look terrified. As if—"

"It was all an act," Jackie said. "I'm sure she does that all the time. To give people something to talk about and tell their friends."

"Maybe she wanted more money," Judy suggested. "You know. To tell us what the evil was."

"But why did she pick me?" I cried. "Why didn't she tell Jilly she was evil? Or Judy?"

"Because it's your birthday!" Jackie teased.

And then I had a thought. "You set this up—didn't you!" I cried. "You went to the fortune-teller earlier and told her to say that to me!"

"No—" Jackie started. "Really—"

"Yes! You know I always fall for these things!" I insisted. "It's another one of your tricks. But I'm the new Maggie. I'm not going to fall for your little joke."

"We didn't set it up! Honest!" Jilly said, raising her right hand as if swearing an oath.

"I've never seen that woman before!" Jackie declared.

"Come on. Let's forget about it. Let's go on the Ferris wheel," Judy said.

"When we're up at the top, we can lean over and spit on Miss Elizabeth's tent!" Jackie said.

"No. I really want to get away from here." I shuddered. "Really. Let's go. I don't know what to think about that crazy woman. I just want to go."

Jackie put her hands on my shoulders. "You're shaking!" she said. "You didn't take that woman seriously—did you, Maggie? She's crazy!"

"I know. I know," I muttered.

But as we walked back to the Mullens' house, I kept examining my palm. I couldn't get that woman and her frightened face and her terrified cries out of my mind.

As soon as we got inside, we ordered pizza. Then I pulled out the magic kit my mom bought me for my birthday. And I started doing some of the tricks.

"Watch carefully. Which hand is the coin in?" I

asked, holding my closed fists in front of them.

Jackie rolled her eyes. "Your mother bought you this?"

I nodded. "Come on. Which hand?"

"Your mother must think you're five years old!" Jackie said.

"I had that same kit when I was seven," Judy chimed in.

"But you know I'm really into this stuff!" I protested. "You know I love magic. Check this out." I shoved the box in front of them. "The disappearing dollar-bill trick. And remember this one with the cups and the three red balls?"

"You're definitely weird," Jilly said.

"No, I'm not," I replied sharply. The fortune-teller flashed into my mind again. "I just like the idea of making things appear and disappear. I think it's so cool."

"Make the pizza appear," Jilly said. "I'm starving!"

"Okay," I agreed. I waved my hand three times toward the front door. "Pizza—appear!" I command-ed in a deep voice.

And the doorbell buzzed.

Everyone laughed in surprise. "Yaay! You did it!" Jilly cried. She ran to the front door to get it.

"What did your father send you for your birth-day?" Jackie asked.

I sighed. "He forgot again, I guess. He didn't call."

My parents have been divorced since I was four. My dad lives in Seattle, and he doesn't call that much.

I took out a silvery box from the magic kit. "Here. Let me show you a great trick before we eat. Jackie, lend me your necklace."

Jackie's smile faded. "My necklace?" She reached a hand up to the tiny, brightly colored glass beads.

"Yeah. Just lend it to me for a minute," I said, holding my hand out for it. "This is a really cool trick. You'll be amazed. Really."

She frowned. "Be careful, okay, Maggie?" She bent her head and started to slide the necklace off. "You know how much this necklace means to me. My great-grandmother gave it to me. I never take it off."

"She didn't give me anything," Judy griped.

"She didn't like you," Jackie snapped. The beads caught in her long, black hair. She carefully tugged them free and handed the necklace to me.

"Wow. It's so light and delicate," I said. "Now, watch carefully."

I slid open the silver box and carefully tucked the necklace inside. Then I turned the box over and over between my hands. "You watching?" I asked.

"Yeah. Sure," Jackie replied. Judy stared at the box without blinking. Jilly set the pizza down on the coffee table and watched the box twirl in my hands.

"This box leads to the fourth dimension," I

announced. "When I open it up, your necklace will not be inside. It will be in the fourth dimension."

"Jilly lives in the fourth dimension!" Jackie said. Judy laughed. Jilly stuck her tongue out at Jackie.

"The necklace is gone!" I declared. I slid open the box and showed them it was empty.

"Cool!" Jilly said.

"Good trick," Jackie said. "Very good."

I slid the box shut again. Then I turned it over. "Necklace—return from the fourth dimension!" I ordered.

I pulled open the box and peered inside. "Hey—!"

"It's not there," Jackie said.

"Whoa. Wait a minute," I said. I turned the box again and slid open the lid. "No. Not there. Hold on."

I raised my eyes to Jackie. She was glaring at me impatiently. "Maggie—?"

My chin trembled. "It's in here. I know it is!"

I turned the box and opened it again. No. I opened both sides. I slid open the secret compartment. No.

"Oh, wow!" I cried. "Oh, wow. Jackie—I—I'm so sorry! I don't know where it went!"

With an angry cry Jackie jumped up from the couch. She grabbed the box from my hands and examined it. "Maggie, is this some kind of a joke?"

I couldn't keep up the act any longer. I laughed. "Of course it is!" I exclaimed. "It's a magic trick—right? Look in your pocket."

Jackie squinted at me suspiciously. "Huh?"

I pointed. "Look in your pocket."

She reached into her T-shirt pocket and pulled out the necklace.

"Wow!" Judy clapped her hands.

"That's so totally wild!" Jilly declared. "You're good, Maggie. You're really good!"

I took a quick bow.

But then I saw Jackie still glaring at me. "I think it was mean," she said through her teeth. She carefully returned the necklace to her neck.

"It was just a trick!" I protested. "Besides, it's not as mean as making someone's pants fall down!"

"But you know how much this necklace means to

me," Jackie said. "It's the most beautiful thing I own."

"Yes, it's beautiful," I agreed. I sighed. "I wish I had one like it. I'd never take mine off, either."

Jackie eyed me suspiciously. Finally a smile crossed her lips. "Well, if it ever really disappears, I'll know who swiped it!"

I laughed at that, along with Judy and Jilly.

I had no way of knowing that Jackie's necklace would disappear for real just a few days later.

Jilly brought paper plates and cans of Diet Coke from the kitchen. We each took pizza slices and carried them back to the living room to chow down.

"Maggie, do another trick," Jilly urged.

"No. Turn on the TV," Judy said. "See if there are any good movies on."

Jackie glanced at the clock on the mantel. "It's pretty late," she said to me. "Think you should call your mom or something? Tell her you're still here?"

"No. She had to work tonight," I replied. My mom is a nurse at Cedar Bay General. She has a different work schedule every week.

I started to lift my pizza slice to my mouth— when I felt a hard bump—like a heavy brick landing on my lap. "Plumper!" I cried. The pizza slice started to fall. I made a wild grab for it.

Judy's enormous orange-and-white cat pushed its fat body against my side.

"Plumper—get down!" Judy ordered. "Get off Maggie!"

Of course the cat ignored her.

The cat burrowed its fat head into my lap. "I don't believe this!" I cried to Judy. "Why does he always pick on me?"

"Plumper knows you don't like him," Judy replied.

"He's just so big and heavy, and he always jumps on me, and—and—" I sneezed hard. Once. And then sneezed again.

"You don't have to sneeze like that. We know you're allergic to cats!" Jackie said.

"Oh, yuck!" I cried. I held up my pizza slice. It had clumps of orange fur stuck all over it.

The cat stretched its paws over my lap.

"Plumper—what did you do?" Judy scolded. "Just shove him away, Maggie. You've got to be firm. Just push him."

I hesitated. I felt about to sneeze again. The cat was so heavy on my lap. Finally I gave him a soft shove. "Go away, Plumper. Go."

To my surprise, he tossed back his head, bared his teeth, and let out a long, frightening hiss.

Before I could move, the big cat swiped its claws over my arm.

"Owww!" I let out a scream. The pizza slice fell to the floor.

The cat hissed again, louder. It lowered its head—

and tried to sink its teeth into my arm.

With a cry, I leaped up.

I tried to back away, but stumbled over the coffee table.

Hissing furiously, the cat dived for me. Swiped both front paws over my jeans legs, clawing, snapping its jaws.

I fell hard onto my back. And before I could roll or spin away, the cat was on top of me. Hissing so loudly, so furiously. Hissing like an angry snake. And clawing, clawing at my face. Climbing over me. Clawing. Biting.

"Help me!" I shrieked. "Help! He's trying to kill me!"

"Plumper!" I could hear Judy scream. She sounded so far away. "Plumper—what's wrong with you!"

I raised both arms to protect my face.

The cat furiously clawed at my sleeves. Snapping. Crying. Hissing with such anger.

Judy grabbed the cat. Tossed him over her shoulder. And hurried out of the room, holding him like a big bag of laundry.

"Ohhhh." I let out a groan.

I struggled slowly to my feet. My whole body trembled.

"I never saw Plumper do that before!" Jilly declared, taking my arm.

Jackie hurried over to me. "Are you okay? Maggie? Are you cut?"

31

I checked myself out. My clothes were covered in orange fur. "I—I guess I'm all right," I said shakily.

"You have a small scratch on your hand," Jackie reported, checking me out. "But he didn't break the skin."

"Stupid, crazy cat," Jilly muttered. She started to pull clumps of fur off me.

Judy returned, shaking her head, pulling cat fur off her sweater. "I had to lock him in the back. That was so weird!"

"He's never done anything like that before," Jilly said. "He's always just fat, lazy, and contented."

"So why did he go berserk and attack Maggie like that?" Judy asked, her voice trembling.

Jackie's dark eyes lit up. "Because Maggie is evil!" she declared. "EVIL!"

Her two sisters laughed.

But I didn't think it was funny.

"I'm not evil!" I protested shrilly. "That cat is evil!"

"I'll keep him away from you from now on," Judy promised, biting her bottom lip. "I—I don't know what made him do that. He just went . . . nuts. It's so weird. So weird . . ."

I turned and saw Jackie staring at me, studying me intently. "What are you thinking?" I demanded.

She blinked. "Nothing," she said. "Nothing at all."

I left their house a few minutes later. I didn't feel like eating pizza anymore. I kept picturing the slice with the orange fur stuck in the sauce.

The night air had cooled off a bit, but it still felt heavy and damp. Yellow-gray clouds covered the sky, hiding the moon and stars.

I still felt shaky as I turned toward my house. My

shoes scraped the sidewalk as I walked, the only sound except for the soft whisper of the trees.

That was so horrifying! I thought. The cat always sat in my lap before. Why did it decide to attack me tonight?

"Because you're EVIL!" Jackie had said.

It wasn't funny. It was so totally insane.

I'm not evil. I've never done anything evil. In fact, I'm the least evil person I know!

Jackie is more evil than I am, I told myself. She is. She definitely has a mean sense of humor.

Rigging Glen's Tarzan costume like that. Embarrassing him in front of the whole school. Pretending she was going to force me to get a tattoo tonight.

That's really evil.

Well . . . no.

I changed my mind. It's not evil. It's . . . mischievous, that's all.

Was tonight another one of Jackie's "mischievous" jokes? I wondered. Did she pay Miss Elizabeth to say those things about me? Jackie swore she didn't.

I thought about the fortune-teller. Pictured her solemn face again, leaning into the red glow of her crystal ball.

Why did she say I was evil? Why did she say that about me?

Why did she pick me?

Ask her, I thought. Just ask her, Maggie.

Make her explain. Then you'll never have to think about it again.

I stopped at the corner. A car rolled past, music blaring from the open window. I waited for it to pass, then took a few more steps—and stopped in the middle of the street.

My house was one block away. The carnival at the pier was four blocks in the other direction.

Go ahead, I urged myself. Go to the carnival. Get it out of your mind for good.

"Okay, I'm going," I whispered. I turned and started toward the pier.

I'm going to tell Miss Elizabeth how cruel that was, I decided. I'm going to tell her that she ruined my birthday with that lame act.

Another car rolled past, this one filled with teenagers. A boy yelled something out the window. I ignored him and kept walking.

I stopped under a streetlamp to check my watch. A little before midnight. My mom would probably kill me if she knew I was walking around by myself this late.

"Hey, I'm thirteen now," I said out loud. "I'm not a kid."

The carnival was probably closing down. I hoped Miss Elizabeth was still there. I began to feel angrier and angrier. People go to a carnival for fun—not to be frightened or insulted.

A strong wind came up, blowing against me, pushing me back. I leaned into it and kept going.

I reached the pier. It was nearly deserted. A few couples were leaving the carnival, carrying armloads of stuffed-animal prizes. The ticket booth stood empty. The entrance gate was open.

As I stepped through it, all of the lights dimmed. I blinked in the sudden darkness.

An empty Pepsi can rattled over the ground in a gust of wind. It rolled at my feet and I jumped over it.

The carnival music had been turned off, but the loudspeakers crackled with static. And over the sound of the static, I could hear the steady slap of water against the pier.

Workers closed up the game booths. Most of the booths were already dark and deserted. A young man was pulling a wooden gate over the front of his booth. He looked up when he saw me walk past. "Hey—we're closed," he called.

"I know," I called back. "I'm . . . uh . . . looking for somebody."

The crackling static in the loudspeakers grew louder as I made my way to the end of the pier. From nearby I heard a low howl.

An animal howl?

The wind through the pier planks?

More lights flickered out. Darkness washed over me. Someone in the distance laughed, a high, cold laugh.

I shivered. Maybe this was a mistake.

I heard scraping footsteps behind me.

I spun around. Just dead brown leaves, scuttling on the pier in a swirl of wind.

The empty cars on the roller-coaster track gleamed dully in the dim light. I heard a squeaking sound. The tracks rattled as if being shaken.

Finally the fortune-teller's tent came into view at the end of the pier.

I swallowed hard. My heart began to race.

I stopped outside the entrance. The tent flap had been pulled shut. Was she in there?

I had been rehearsing what I'd say to Miss Elizabeth. But now it all flew out of my mind.

I'll just ask her why she said that about me, I decided. That's all. I'll just ask her why.

I took a deep breath. Then I grabbed the tent flap with both hands and pulled it open.

"Hello?" I called in. My voice sounded tiny. "Anyone in here? Miss Elizabeth? Are you here?"

No answer.

I stepped inside—and let out a shocked gasp.

One of the two lanterns remained on the tent wall, casting the only light. I spotted the other lantern, the glass cracked, on its side on the ground.

The wooden table was overturned. A leg broken off.

Next to it, one of the fortune-teller's long, silky scarves lay torn and crumpled into a ball.

The chairs—the two wooden chairs were splintered and broken. The poster of the human hand had been ripped in half.

And the red glass ball—shattered—shards of broken glass over the tent floor. The ball—the crystal ball—smashed into a thousand pieces.

The next day in school I tried to shut the fortune-teller out of my mind. After school there was no time to think about her. I had a dance class.

Jilly was there, too. I watched her in awe. She is such a graceful dancer. She seems to float over the floor.

Dancing beside her, I felt like a circus elephant.

I can't compete with Jilly. But I'm going to the dance tryouts anyway, I decided. It's my dream to make that company. I'm not going to give up without trying.

I hurried home after the class. I had piles of homework.

It was a cool autumn day. The air smelled sweet and fresh as I jogged onto my block. I waved to some kids raking leaves on their driveway.

I stopped short when I reached my front yard. The backpack bounced heavily on my back.

Was I seeing things?

Or was that really Glen pushing the power lawn

mower over our front lawn?

"Hey—!" I called to him and waved.

He spun around. The mower roared. He cut the engine. "Maggie—what's up?" he called.

I ran over to him. "What are you doing?" I called. Dumb question. I felt my face grow hot and knew I was blushing.

He wiped sweat off his forehead with the sleeve of his gray jacket. "I mow all the lawns on this block," he said. "Didn't you ever see me?"

I shook my head.

"Your mom asked me to cut yours before winter comes." He wiped his hands on his jeans legs. "The mower keeps conking out. I don't know what its problem is." He kicked it with his sneaker.

It was chilly out, but he was sweating a lot. His curly hair—wild and unbrushed as always—glistened with sweat. I reached out and pulled a blade of grass off his cheek.

"Nice house." He pointed. "You could fit my house in there about ten times!"

"You want to come in?" I blurted out. "I mean— if you're thirsty or something. Come in and have a Coke or some Gatorade. When you finish mowing?"

He nodded. "Yeah. Maybe. Thanks. I have another lawn to do before dark." He bent to start the mower up. "Catch you later."

I hurried into the house. "He's definitely cool," I murmured. I stepped inside and called out,

"Mom—are you home?"

Silence.

I never can keep her work schedule straight.

I grabbed a can of iced tea from the fridge and made my way up to my room to start my homework. Chirpy, my canary, started chirping away as soon as I entered the room. I walked over to her cage in front of the window and rubbed her yellow feathered back with one finger.

And peeked out at Glen down below. He was leaning over the mower handlebars, moving quickly, making stripes across the grass. "So cute," I muttered to Chirpy. "Don't you think he's cute?"

The canary tilted her head to one side, trying to understand.

I trotted to the mirror and brushed my hair. Then I put on some lip gloss and a little eye makeup.

I decided to change. I pulled on a fresh pair of straight-leg jeans and my new white sweater.

I could hear the hum and roar of the mower outside. Wish Glen would hurry up and finish, I thought.

I knew I should start my homework. But I couldn't concentrate.

I went back to the window and watched him for a while. Then I picked up a deck of cards and started to practice a few new tricks. But I couldn't concentrate on those, either.

I heard voices outside. Girls' voices.

41

"Hey, Tarzan!" someone yelled.

I dived back to the window and saw Jackie and Judy coming up the driveway. They had stopped to tease Glen.

He just kept mowing. I could see that his face was bright red, and he was pretending to ignore them.

"Give him a break!" I said out loud. I hurried downstairs to let them in.

"Whoa. Way to go, Maggie. You got your boyfriend to mow the lawn!" Jackie teased.

"Mom hired him," I replied. "I didn't even know—"

"Were you in chem lab when Kenny Fields dropped the glass beaker?" Judy interrupted.

"No. I don't have lab on Monday," I said.

"It was a disaster!" she exclaimed. "It was some kind of ammonia or smelly acid—something really gross. It smelled so horrible, kids started to puke all over the place."

"First, one kid hurled, and then everyone was hurling," Jackie said. "It was awesome! Like an epidemic!"

"They had to evacuate half the school," Judy said. "How come you didn't know?"

"I wasn't there. We had a dumb field trip," I said, rolling my eyes. "To the art museum."

"Why don't you invite your boyfriend in?" Jackie asked.

"I already did," I told them. I could hear the

mower's roar, fainter now. Glen was nearly down to the curb.

Jackie pushed past me and started to the stairs. "I want to try all those new cosmetics you bought at the mall."

Judy and I followed her. "Where's Jilly?" I asked.

"More dance practice," Judy said. "She took an extra class today. She really wants to be perfect at that audition."

I sighed. "She already is perfect."

Jackie went right to my dresser. "It's like a make-up store in here!" she declared. She started picking up jars and tubes and examining them. "This is totally cool."

"If you're going to try all my makeup, you have to give me something in return," I said.

Jackie laughed. "Okay. I'll give you Jilly!"

"Ha ha," I said. I reached out my hand. "Let me try on your necklace."

Jackie hesitated.

"Just for a minute," I said. "You've never let me try it on. I just want to see how it looks on me."

Jackie shrugged and carefully pulled off the necklace of tiny glass beads. "No magic tricks?"

"No magic tricks," I promised.

She handed it to me and went back to pawing over all my new makeup.

"It's so beautiful," I said, gazing into the mirror, adjusting the delicate, sparkling beads around my throat. "I'd do anything to have one just like it."

I caught Jackie's smile in the mirror. "Anything?"

"Well . . ."

"Maybe I'll leave it to you in my will," Jackie said.

"Do you have a lot of homework?" Judy asked.

"Tons," I said, sighing. "I tried getting started on it when I got home. But my mind kept spinning. I couldn't concentrate."

Judy stood at the birdcage, petting Chirpy. She narrowed her eyes at me. "You're not still upset about that fortune-teller, are you?"

I laughed. "Thanks a bunch, Judy. Thanks for reminding me. I haven't thought about that all day!"

"You're evil," Jackie muttered, brushing thick, black mascara on her lashes. "You're so evil, Maggie."

"Shut up," I snapped. "That was totally dumb, and you know it. I don't know why I let it upset me."

Judy opened the cage and gently lifted Chirpy out. She let the canary perch on her finger. "Plumper would love you," Judy told the bird. "For lunch!"

"Don't mention that cat to me!" I cried. "That was so horrible! Your cat is a psycho!"

Judy frowned. "I'm really sorry about that. You know, I came over to ask if you'd help me with the Pet Fair."

"Not if I have to go near that cat!" I said.

"I'll keep Plumper away," Judy promised. "Will you help out?"

"I guess," I replied.

I glanced out the window. What's taking Glen so long? I wondered. Why doesn't he get finished?

Watching him moving back and forth, back and forth, I silently wished there was a way to speed up his mower.

"Hey—!" Judy's startled cry interrupted my thoughts. I spun around to see Chirpy fluttering in the air.

Judy grabbed at the canary with both hands. "Come back! Come back here, birdy!"

Chirping loudly, the canary flew up to the ceiling, hit the ceiling light, bounced off, and flew to the closet.

Judy and I both chased after him. "Come back!" I cried. "What's wrong with you?"

All three of us tried to grab the flittering, fluttering bird. Each time we nearly had her, Chirpy darted out of our reach.

At first it was kind of funny. But after ten minutes of chasing after the bird, it wasn't funny anymore. It was just frustrating.

"I don't believe this!" I cried breathlessly. I made another grab for the bird—and just missed! "Chirpy—stop it! You've never done this before! Come back! I could kill you for this!"

"Whoa. Don't say that!" Jackie declared. "Wouldn't you feel terrible if you said that and then Chirpy died?"

"I didn't mean it. It's just a stupid expression," I said. I stopped to catch my breath.

And Chirpy flew into her cage.

Judy slammed the cage door shut. "Gotcha!"

I was still breathing hard. I suddenly realized I still had Jackie's necklace around my neck. I took it off and handed it to her.

"Why don't we go down to the kitchen—" I started to say. But that's as far as I got. Because we all heard a scream of alarm from outside.

I dived to the window with Judy and Jackie right behind me. Peering out, I saw Glen chasing after his lawn mower. The mower was zigzagging wildly, roaring away from him. He was running after it full speed, shouting his head off.

My heart pounding, I shoved open the window. "Glen—!" I called. "What's happening?"

I don't think he could hear me over the roar of the mower.

He lunged forward and grabbed the handle. But the mower jerked away from him.

"Hey—helllp!" he shouted.

Jackie and Judy both giggled beside me. But I could see that Glen was really struggling, and very upset.

He grabbed the mower handle again and held on for dear life. But the mower roared forward, digging deep holes in the lawn.

Glen tried frantically to pull it to a stop. But the

mower zigzagged crazily, out of control, pulling Glen with it.

I slapped my hands to my ears as the mower shot into a tree with a deafening crash. It hit so hard, the whole tree shook.

I saw Glen hit the ground. He landed on his back.

And then over the roaring whine of the mower, I heard Glen's horrified shriek:

"My foot! IT CUT OFF MY FOOT!"

"Nooooo!" I let out a scream and pushed away from the window.

All three of us went flying down the stairs—and out to the front yard.

"Glen—are you okay?" I screamed.

He was sitting on the grass, hunched over. He had his shoe off and was rubbing his left foot with both hands. As we ran down to him, the mower rocked against the tree, sputtered, and died.

"Your foot—?" I gasped.

"Sorry. I panicked a little," he said softly. "It's just a small cut. It hurt so much, I thought—"

"False alarm," Jackie said. "You scared us to death!"

"But what happened?" Judy asked.

"Beats me," Glen replied. "I don't understand it at all."

"Did you turn up the speed or something?" Judy asked.

He shook his head. "It just took off. It was so . . .

freaky! It . . . it's impossible! Lawn mowers aren't built to go that fast!"

He carefully slipped his shoe on and climbed to his feet. He took a few steps, testing his foot. "It's okay," he said.

He wiped sweat off his forehead, then raised his eyes to the mower. It had shot into the tree so hard, it left a deep gash in the tree trunk.

"Wow," Glen muttered. "Weird."

He made his way to the mower and wrapped his hands around the handles. He pulled it slowly off the tree. Then he turned to me. "Tell your mom I'm sorry, okay? The mower made a real mess here."

"Okay, I'll tell her," I said. "But—"

"Tell her I'll get the mower fixed and come back." He started to push it to the driveway.

"Don't you want to come in for a minute?" I asked. "Get something to drink?"

He pushed back his bushy hair. "No. I'd better get this thing home so my dad can look at it. Maybe he can figure out why it went berserk. See you."

I watched Glen push the mower down the driveway to the sidewalk. Then I turned and followed Jackie and Judy back into the house.

As we stepped inside, Jackie snickered.

"That was so scary!" I said. "What's so funny?"

Jackie's eyes flashed. "I thought you liked Glen, Maggie. Did you use your evil powers on his lawn mower?" She laughed.

49

"Stop it!" I cried angrily. "I mean it, Jackie. Stop saying that! You know I don't have evil powers! So stop it! It isn't funny!"

Her eyes went wide. I could see she was surprised by how angry I got.

"Sorry," she whispered. "I didn't mean it. I was only joking. Really. I was just trying to lighten up—"

"Well, don't!" I interrupted.

She put a hand on my shoulder. "I'll never mention it again. Promise."

We made our way back upstairs. The window was still open, and a cold wind filled my bedroom. The curtains fluttered and flapped.

I moved to close the window, but stopped halfway across the room.

A tiny yellow feather floated in the air in front of me.

I turned. And stared at the birdcage.

Stared at Chirpy. Stared at my canary, lying so still . . . so still.

Dead on her side on the floor of the cage.

When I got over the shock, Judy helped me wrap the poor little bird in tissue paper. I carried him out behind the garage. Jackie dug a shallow hole in the soft dirt back there. And we buried Chirpy.

We stood silently, staring down at the little grave. All three of us felt weird. Especially Judy, who loves animals so much.

Jackie kept her promise and didn't say anything about evil powers. I think we were all thinking the same thing. When I was chasing Chirpy around the room, I shouted, "I could kill you for this."

And a few minutes later the little canary lay stiff and dead.

But no one believed that I was really responsible. And for once, Jackie didn't joke about it.

The afternoon sun began to set behind the trees. I shivered as the air grew colder. Fat brown leaves fell from the trees, scattering over the freshly cut lawn.

My friends and I were returning to the house when I saw Mom's brown Taurus pull up the driveway. Jackie and Judy lingered behind, but I went running to meet the car.

"What are you three doing out here without jackets?" Mom asked. She climbed out of the car and straightened the skirt of her white nurse's uniform. "And what happened to the front lawn? Why is it so torn up?"

"It's a long story," I said, sighing.

As we walked into the house, I told her about Chirpy and about Glen and his runaway lawn mower.

Mom tsk-tsked. She dropped her pocketbook onto the kitchen counter and gazed at me. "That's so strange about Chirpy," she said. "The bird was only a year old."

Jackie hoisted her backpack off the floor. "Judy and I should be going. It's getting late."

"I have tons of homework, too," Judy said to me. "It's like they all piled it on today."

"I guess the bird got overexcited, flying around your room like that," Mom said. She tossed her coat on a kitchen stool. "Probably had a heart attack."

She carried the teakettle to the sink and filled it with water. "Sure you girls don't want to stay and have something hot to drink?"

"No. Thanks. We really have to go," Jackie said.

I followed them to the front.

We were passing the bookshelves in the front hallway when Jackie suddenly stopped. She stooped down and examined the bottom shelf of books. "Whoa. Maggie—what's this?"

"Huh?" I knelt down beside her to see what had caught her eye. The shelf was filled with old books, the covers frayed and faded. "What about them—?" I started to ask.

But then I read some of the titles. And I saw what the old books were about. Witchcraft . . . the Dark Arts . . . Magic . . . and the Occult.

"I—I've never noticed these down here before," I said.

Jackie stared hard at me.

"Big deal," I said sharply. "So, it's a bunch of old books. Why are you looking at me like that?"

Jackie shrugged. Then she climbed quickly to her feet and gave Judy a shove toward the front door. "Call you after dinner," she said.

"Bye," Judy said. "Sorry about your canary. She was sweet."

I closed the front door after them and turned to find Mom in the hallway.

"Mom, can I ask you something?" I said. I knew it was crazy and stupid. I knew it was totally ridiculous. But the question just popped out of my mouth.

"Mom, am I weird? Do I have some kind of evil powers?"

She narrowed her eyes at me. She took a breath. "Well . . . yes," she said finally. "Yes, you do."

"Huh?" I gasped. I could feel my heart skip a beat.

"Yes," Mom said. "And every night after you go to sleep, I take out my broomstick and fly to Cleveland!"

She laughed.

I just stared at her with my mouth hanging open.

She wrapped her hand tenderly around the back of my neck, the way she used to do when I was little. "Maggie, why on earth would you ask such a crazy question?"

I swallowed hard. "Well . . ." I hesitated. Then I figured I might as well go ahead and explain.

So I told her about the fortune-teller at the carnival and about how Jackie had been teasing me ever since. And how Judy's cat suddenly attacked me for no reason.

"You know you're perfectly normal, Maggie," Mom said. "You know you're not a witch or anything."

"I know, Mom, but—"

"Besides, if you have these evil powers, why didn't you use them before?" Mom asked. "Why did you start two nights ago? You went thirteen years, and now all of a sudden you're evil?"

"You're right," I said. "I don't know why that woman at the carnival got me so upset."

"She was just having her little joke," Mom said. "What happened to your sense of humor, Maggie? You've gotten very serious lately. You've got to lighten up."

I started to agree again. But then the bottom shelf of books caught my eye. "Mom—" I pointed. "Those books . . ."

Mom sighed. She squeezed my neck again. "I wrote my senior paper on strange beliefs. I told you that. Remember? I've had those old books since college."

"Oh. Right."

Now I really felt stupid. "Sorry, Mom. I'll never mention the whole thing again. I knew it was dumb. But—"

My phone rang upstairs in my room. "I'd better get that. Call me for dinner," I said, and I hurtled up the stairs two at a time.

I grabbed the phone after the third ring, and panted, "Hello?"

It was Jackie on the other end of the line, and she sounded frantic. "My necklace—" she choked out. "You forgot to give it back."

"Huh? No," I protested. "I handed it to you. Don't you remember?"

"You couldn't have returned it!" she screeched. "I don't have it!"

"Calm down, Jackie," I said softly. "I know I gave it to you. Let's try to think—"

"I don't have it!" Jackie repeated shrilly. "It's not in my coat or in my backpack. It's got to be some-where in your room, Maggie. Look for it—okay? Look for it."

"Yeah. Sure." I turned and glanced quickly around my room. No necklace on the dresser . . . the bed . . . the desk . . .

I tried to picture Jackie as she left the house. She was wearing the necklace. I was sure she had it around her neck.

"I—I don't see it," I told her. "You were wearing it. I know you were."

"Find it!" Jackie shrieked. "You've got to find it! Find it, Maggie—please!"

The next morning at school between classes, I ran into Glen. "Where are you going?" I asked.

"Gym," he said. "How about you?"

"Spanish." I yawned. "How's your foot?"

"It's okay." He grinned. "I was lucky. I still have all six toes!"

We bumped through the crowd. Cedar Bay Middle School is too small. Between classes the halls look like cattle stampedes.

I yawned again. "Sorry. I stayed up past midnight doing homework." I shook my head. "I'm in great shape for the dance tryouts tonight. I'll probably yawn in the judges' faces."

Glen shifted his backpack on his shoulders. "Are you nervous?"

"Yes," I admitted. "Even though I know I don't stand much of a chance. Jilly is so much better than me. She's an awesome dancer."

Glen nodded thoughtfully. Then he reached out and solemnly shook my hand. "Good luck," he said. "Break a leg."

I laughed. "I think you say that to actors. I don't think that's the right thing to say to a dancer."

He turned the corner and gave me a little wave. "Catch you later."

I followed the crowd, thinking about the dance tryout. Why am I even bothering? I asked myself.

I answered my own question: Because it's the new, bold me.

I vowed on my birthday that I would change. That I wouldn't be so shy, so timid. That I would go after what I really wanted.

And that's why I had no choice. I had to go to that dance audition after dinner.

I turned a corner and headed to the stairs. I was on the second floor. My Spanish class was in the language lab on the first floor.

I grabbed the railing and started down the steep, tile stairs. I had only taken a step or two when I spotted Jilly halfway down the stairs.

Suddenly I had the strangest feeling. My arms started to tingle. My hands felt all prickly, as if they'd fallen asleep. And then my hands started to burn. They were burning hot.

I tried to ignore it. "Hey, Jilly—!" I called. But she didn't hear me. I elbowed my way through the students.

"Jilly." I tapped her lightly on the shoulder—and I saw her hands fly up like two birds taking flight.

Then I saw her shoes slide off the step.

And I saw her eyes go wide and her mouth pull open. Her shrill scream rang through the stairwell.

And she fell. Fell forward. Her hair flying behind her.

Jilly swooped straight down. Down . . . down . . . bumping the hard tile stairs.

Thud . . . thud . . . thud . . . thud . . .

Screaming all the way down.

She landed hard. I saw her head bounce against the floor.

She uttered one last groan.

And then she didn't move.

My knees started to crumple. I gripped the railing to hold myself up.

"Nooooo!" I wailed. "Jilly? Jilly—?"

She lay sprawled on her stomach at the bottom of the stairs, one arm tucked under her body, the other straight out. Her hair had come loose and spread over her head, hiding her face like a furry yellow blanket.

"Jilly—? Jilly—?" I shouted her name as I ran down the stairs.

She raised her head off the floor. "Why . . . why did you push me?" she choked out.

"Huh? I didn't push you!" I cried. "I just tapped you!"

Jilly pulled herself to a sitting position. She had a cut on her shoulder. It was bleeding through her white top.

Her eyes remained locked on me. "Yes, you did. You pushed me, Maggie."

"No—!" I cried. Some kids had stopped to help

Jilly. Now they were all staring at me. "No. I didn't touch you. You know I wouldn't push you. I—I called out, and then—"

She rubbed her sweater, feeling the dampness of the blood. "You—you're lying. I felt your hand on my back. You shoved me. I felt you shove me, Maggie."

"N-no," I protested. "I swear. I didn't touch you. You just fell."

Everyone stared hard at me now. I could feel their accusing eyes.

Why didn't they just go away? Why didn't they all go to class?

I turned and saw that Jilly's leg was cut too.

"Hey—!" I cried. "Your shoelace. Jilly—look. Your shoelace is untied."

She groaned and rubbed her side. "Huh?" She squinted at her shoe.

"See?" I said. "That must be it. That must be what happened. You tripped over your shoelace."

"You shoved me," she insisted. "I felt you push me. You could have killed me, Maggie. Does the dance tryout mean that much to you? You could have killed me!"

"No," I repeated, shaking my head. "No, no, no."

We were such good friends. Why was she accusing me?

I didn't push her. I know I didn't.

• • •

After school I hurried over to the Mullens' house to see if Jilly was okay.

Judy answered the door. "Oh. It's you!" She seemed surprised to see me.

"Is Jilly here?" I asked, following her into the den. "Is she okay?"

The TV was on—some talk show with all the guests screaming at each other. Judy clicked it off.

"Jilly is still at the doctor," Judy said, plopping down on the green leather couch. "She's getting her ankle taped."

"She—she didn't break it—did she?" I asked.

Judy shook her head. "Just a sprain. She'll probably be able to try out tonight."

I let out a long, relieved sigh and dropped into the armchair across from Judy. "I'm so glad she's okay," I said. And then my voice shook: "She—she accused me of pushing her down the stairs. But that's crazy!"

Judy brushed back her short hair. Her eyes were locked on me, studying me intently.

"I didn't push her," I said. "I didn't bump into her, or anything."

I held my breath, waiting for Judy to reply.

Finally she said, "Even if you did bump her, it had to be an accident." She tucked her slender legs beneath her on the couch. "I know you'd never deliberately try to hurt her."

"Of course not," I said. "I'm so glad you believe me. If only—"

I stopped when I heard the front door slam. Jackie came running into the room. Her mouth dropped open when she saw me. "You're here!"

I turned in the chair. "Yes, I—"

"Did you find it?" Jackie demanded breathlessly. "I've been looking for you all day. Did you find my necklace?"

"No," I said. "I searched everywhere. I turned the whole house upside down."

"But—but—" Jackie sputtered. Her long hair was wild and unbrushed. One side stood straight up. Her expression was frantic.

"Then where is it?" she cried. She rubbed a hand over her throat as if she hoped to find it there.

"I even searched behind the garage," I told her. "Where we buried the canary. No sign of it."

"I'm desperate without it," she said. "I'm totally desperate."

"I'm really so sorry," I said, lowering my eyes. "I'll keep looking. I promise."

She shut her eyes and sighed. "It's just so weird."

Then she startled me. She ran across the den, wrapped her arms around me, and hugged me. "I wasn't accusing you, Maggie," she whispered. Her cheek was burning hot against mine. "You know that—right? You're my friend. My best friend."

Without waiting for an answer, she spun away and hurried from the room.

Judy must have seen how stunned I felt. "Jackie

has been a little emotional," she said. "Ever since her necklace disappeared."

I settled back in the armchair. But I didn't have time to relax.

I heard the rapid thud of soft footsteps over the carpet.

And then I let out a frightened cry as Judy's huge cat Plumper leaped onto my lap.

"Get him off!" I shrieked. "Get him off me!"

Judy jumped up. "Plumper—come here!" she called.

But to my surprise, the big orange cat burrowed his face into my chest and purred.

"Judy—" I gasped. "He—he—"

Plumper settled into my lap, purring softly.

"I don't get this," I murmured, still trembling. "One night he tries to claw me to pieces—"

Judy smiled. "He's trying to make up," she said. Her smile grew wider. "Isn't that adorable?"

Purring louder, the cat rubbed its head against my T-shirt.

"Go ahead. Pet him," Judy instructed. "See? He wants you to be nice to him."

I swallowed hard. The cat was so unpredictable. What if I tried to pet him and he started slashing at me again?

"Pet him," Judy urged. "He's waiting for you to pet his fur."

"I—I don't really want to," I said, staring down at

the fat, orange creature.

"He wants you to," Judy replied. "He wants you to make up."

"Well . . ." I took a deep breath. I raised my hand slowly, carefully. And . . .

My hand started to tingle again. Both of my arms were tingling. It felt like a million pinpricks. Once again my hands started to burn.

Why is this happening again? I wondered.

The cat purred.

I lowered my hand and smoothed it gently over Plumper's furry back.

Would he attack? Would he go nuts again?

No. He purred louder.

I rubbed his back. He burrowed his head against me.

"Now you two are friends again," Judy said, beaming happily.

I glanced at the grandfather clock against the wall. "I'd better go," I said. "That dance audition tonight." I gave the cat one more rub. "I hope Jilly and I can be friends again," I said with a sigh.

But Jilly cut me dead at the audition that night.

She glimpsed me standing there in the auditorium aisle. She turned her head and kept walking.

And when I followed after her, begging her to let me talk to her, she pretended I wasn't there.

I felt so bad. I had to fight back the tears.

It was so unfair.

One of my best friends hated me now. And it wasn't my fault in any way.

I could see that she had a slight limp as she climbed onto the bare stage and began to limber up. Her right toe shoe bulged, and I could see that her foot was bandaged beneath her tights.

Ms. Masters, the dance adviser, waved to me to come up to the stage. Then she moved to a CD player on the floor against the curtain and put on some warm-up music.

I sat down on the edge of the stage to tie my ballet slippers. I felt so awkward. I kept glancing at Jilly. She deliberately turned away every time I looked in her direction.

There were only four girls trying out for the one opening in the dance company. Not a big crowd. Just Ms. Masters and four girls onstage. So it would be pretty hard for Jilly and me to ignore each other completely.

My hands fumbled with the laces. I'm too upset to audition, I thought. I'll just leave.

I glanced at Jilly again. She was twirling on her bad foot, testing it.

"Hey, Jilly—looking good!" I called.

She stuck her nose in the air and ignored me.

This is ridiculous! I decided. She has no right to treat me like this.

I'm going to audition. I'm not going to let Jilly drive me away. And I'm going to dance the best I've ever danced!

I finished lacing my toe shoes and hurried onstage to warm up.

Well . . . I didn't exactly dance the best I've ever danced. But I didn't embarrass myself, either.

I was glad when Ms. Masters asked me to try out first. It meant I wouldn't have to stand around and get more and more nervous watching the others.

Jilly and the other two girls—Marci and Deena— had to watch me. And as I danced a short section from *Swan Lake*, I knew they were standing there at the side of the stage, arms crossed in front of them, watching my every move.

But I concentrated on the steps and the music and shut them from my mind.

Afterwards Ms. Masters clapped her hands and smiled. "That was very nice, Maggie," she said. "I'm impressed."

Struggling to catch my breath, I thanked her and padded off, feeling light as a feather, trying to make my exit graceful.

Yes, I knew I had slipped once or twice. And I got behind the music a few times. I guess I was concentrating too hard on the steps, on not messing up.

But over all, I felt pretty good about it. The truth is, it's not easy to get a compliment from Ms. Masters.

Now I leaned against the stage wall and watched as Jilly stepped out, toe shoes tapping the floor so lightly, like little bird feet.

Normally we would have wished each other luck. Normally she would have congratulated me on doing such a good job.

But that was before today. Before . . .

Ms. Masters started the music, and Jilly raised her arms, pasted a smile on her face, and started to dance.

She's a wonderful, graceful dancer. Moving so lightly, so effortlessly, her blond hair tied back, her arms so slow and lovely, she really looks like an angel onstage.

My heart was still pounding from my dance. I wiped perspiration from above my upper lip and watched Jilly.

Such perfect jumps. Such quick feet.

I felt jealous. I couldn't help it. I really, really wanted to be in this dance company. Jilly was into all kinds of activities and clubs and sports at school. But this was the only thing I wanted.

My hands started to tingle and burn. I clasped them tightly together. Why did this keep happening?

Marci, one of the other dancers, leaned close to me. "Wow," she whispered, her eyes on Jilly. "Wow."

I nodded, clasping and unclasping my burning hands.

"We might as well go home," Deena whispered.

Jilly looks so comfortable onstage, I thought. So natural . . . So happy.

But then I saw her expression suddenly change. Her smile faded. She looked surprised. Confused.

All three of us gasped as Jilly started to twirl.

She was near the end of the dance. She had her hands high above her head. As she started to lower them, she raised up on her right foot—and started to spin.

"That's not part of the dance," Marci whispered.

"Is she showing off?" Deena asked.

My arms prickled. I tightened them around myself as I watched Jilly in amazement.

Round and round she twirled. Kicking her left leg out with each spin.

Faster . . . faster . . .

"Unbelievable," Deena said, shaking her head. "What a show-off."

"Wow," Marci repeated.

Jilly twirled even faster now, her arms flying wildly. Her right leg remained stiff and straight as she spun. Her left leg kicked out. Faster . . . harder . . . Her blond ponytail whipped around behind her.

I let out a cry when I caught her expression. Her eyes were wide with fright. Her mouth open in a silent scream, as she spun . . . harder . . . faster . . .

My whole body shuddered in dread. Jilly wasn't showing off.

"She—she can't stop!" I shrieked. "She's out of control!"

My hands burned as if on fire. They throbbed with heat. I clenched my fists tightly, as if trying to keep my hands from exploding! Wave after wave of pain shot up and down my arms.

I gaped in horror as Jilly twirled.

Kick, spin. Kick, spin.

Ms. Masters cut off the music.

But Jilly didn't stop.

Kick, spin. Kick, spin. She hurled herself around and around, her hands flailing.

Silence now. A heavy silence as we all watched in horror.

"Help me—!" Jilly's shrill cry rang out. "Ohhhh, help—!"

And still she spun. Hurling herself harder . . . Hair flying wild now . . . Hands frantically thrashing the air.

"Help me! Pleeeeease!"

And then, still screaming, still moaning in pain, still heaving herself around, Jilly sailed across the stage. Sailed into the wall.

Her body made a sick thud as she hit it.

And then, twirling, still twirling . . . she crumpled to the floor.

"What happened?"

"Why did she do that?"

"Why couldn't she stop?"

"Did she break something? She hit the wall so hard!"

Our frightened voices rang out in the auditorium. We hurried over to Jilly.

Sprawled awkwardly on the stage floor, her eyes shut, her mouth hanging open, legs bent at odd angles, she looked like a broken doll.

"Stand back, everyone," Ms. Masters ordered shrilly. "Stay back. Let me examine her."

"Why was she screaming like that? Why couldn't she stop?" Marci cried. Tears glistened in her eyes.

"Did she lose her balance?" Deena asked, shaking her head. "Did she just spin out of control?"

Holding one hand over my mouth, I stared down at my friend in silence. A heavy feeling of dread rolled over me. My stomach lurched.

"Is—is she breathing?" The question escaped my

lips without my realizing it.

Ms. Masters was down on the floor, bending over Jilly. "Yes, she's breathing," she answered. "Open your eyes, Jilly. Can you open your eyes?"

My eyes moved to Jilly's feet. Her right foot was swelling like a balloon.

My stomach lurched again. I felt really sick.

I swallowed hard several times, forcing my dinner back down.

"Somebody call for an ambulance," Ms. Masters instructed.

"I have a cell phone," Marci said. She ran to get her bag.

"Jilly? Can you hear me?" Ms. Masters asked softly. "Can you open your eyes?"

Jilly finally stirred.

A dry, hacking sound burst from her lips. A gob of saliva ran out of her open mouth, down her cheek.

"Jilly?" Ms. Masters called. "Jilly? Can you hear me?"

Jilly groaned. She blinked several times. "It . . . hurts," she whispered. She moved a hand to her rib cage—then quickly jerked it away. "Ohhhh."

"Lie still," Ms. Masters said. "You might have broken a rib when you crashed into the wall."

Jilly sighed. "Wall?"

"You were spinning so hard," Ms. Masters said. "You lost control and—"

Jilly groaned again. "My foot. I . . . I can't move it."

"Don't try to move anything," the teacher said. "We'll get you to the hospital. You're going to be okay."

"What . . . happened?" Jilly asked groggily. And then suddenly her expression changed. She uttered a sharp gasp as she saw me. Saw me standing there so tensely, my hand still clapped over my mouth.

"Maggie!" she cried hoarsely.

I started toward her, but her cold, angry eyes made me stop.

"Maggie." As she repeated my name, her face twisted in disgust. "You did this!"

"N-no—!" I stammered.

Jilly pointed an accusing finger at me. "I don't know how, but you did this."

Marci and Deena were staring at me.

"Jilly, lie still." Ms. Masters patted Jilly's hand. "I think you've had a concussion. You're confused. No one did anything to you, dear."

"Just like Glen and the lawn mower," Jilly whispered, her finger trembling in the air. "Jackie told me what happened with Glen's lawn mower. The fortune-teller was right. You're evil! You're EVIL!"

"Don't say that!" I screamed. "Jilly—don't! It's not true! You know it's not true! It can't be true! Don't say that!"

Jilly shut her eyes and uttered a moan of pain. "You did this to me! You did it, Maggie!" she whispered.

Her words made everyone turn to me. They were staring at me.

Staring at me as if Jilly had told the truth. As if I really had caused horrible things to happen.

As if I really was evil.

And then, I couldn't hold back. I couldn't hold my hurt, my anger in.

I began screaming at the top of my lungs. Shrieking like an insane person. Screaming at them all:

"I'm not evil! I'm not! I'm not! I'm not!"

A few minutes later the paramedics arrived to take Jilly to the hospital. Ms. Masters hurried out to the hall to phone the Mullens.

Marci and Deena got changed quickly, whispering to themselves. They would have to audition some other time. They kept glancing over at me, but they didn't talk to me.

I changed into my shoes and pulled a jacket over my leotard and tights. I just wanted to get out of there. To get away from their whispers and suspicious looks.

How could Jilly say such a thing about me? How could she blame me like that?

We've been friends since fourth grade. She knows me so well.

She knows I wouldn't hurt her.

I stared at my hands. They didn't burn anymore. Why did that happen again? I wondered.

Every time my hands start to burn, something terrible happens. Every time. But that doesn't mean I'm causing these things to happen—does it?

I shoved my hands into my pockets. I didn't want to think about that. I jumped down from the stage and ran up the auditorium aisle to the exit. I couldn't wait to get home, to the safety of my room.

But Ms. Masters stopped me in the hall. She put a hand on my shoulder. "Jilly was just upset," she said softly. "She didn't mean the crazy things she said."

"I . . . I know," I whispered.

"She must have been in shock," Ms. Masters said. "That's the only explanation."

I nodded.

"Try to put it out of your mind, Maggie. Jilly probably won't even remember she said those things later."

"Probably," I repeated. I grabbed her arm. "But what did happen out there, Ms. Masters? Why did Jilly spin out of control like that?"

My voice shook. "It . . , it was so horrible . . . so frightening. It really looked as if . . . as if some force was controlling her!"

Ms. Masters shook her head. "I'm not sure what happened, Maggie. I think I'm still in shock, too."

She patted my shoulder. "I guess this means you'll be in the dance company. Deena and Marci will have their auditions. But they're not at your level. I'd say congratulations. But I know you're upset about your friend."

"Yes." I nodded again.

A thin smile crossed the teacher's face. "Well, congratulations anyway. We'll celebrate some other time, okay?"

"Thanks, Ms. Masters." I turned and jogged away.

"Try not to think about what Jilly said," she called after me. "She was in shock. I'm sure she'll apologize when she's better."

"Sure," I muttered.

And then I was out of the building. Into the cold, fresh night air. Pale silver moonlight washed over the school grounds. Dead leaves danced across the grass.

I felt like tossing back my head and screaming. I felt like crying.

Instead, I lowered my head into the wind and started running. I didn't go far. I was almost to the corner when I ran right into someone.

"Hey—!" He uttered a startled cry and leaped to the side. "Slow down."

"Glen!" I cried. "What are you doing here?"

He pushed back his wild mop of hair and smiled at me. "Wow. You should try out for track, Maggie."

"Sorry. I didn't see you. I—I wasn't watching. I mean . . . What are you doing here?" I repeated breathlessly.

"Following you," he said.

I gaped at him. "Huh?"

He laughed. "No. I'm kidding. I was down the block, collecting money from people. For mowing their lawns. And I remembered you had that dance thing tonight. So I thought—"

"Don't ask me about it," I said, shuddering. "It was horrible." I started to walk, heading toward home.

He hurried to keep up with me. "You didn't get in?"

"I did get in," I replied. "But—but—" And then I blurted it out. "Jilly got hurt, and she blamed me."

He jumped in front of me to block my path. "Whoa. What happened? You tripped her or something?"

"No. I didn't push her," I said. My voice trembled. I felt about to cry again. "I didn't push her. But she broke her ankle, and she blamed me. Just like this morning at school. She fell down the stairs and blamed me for that. I didn't push her. Really!"

Glen knotted up his face, trying to sort out what I was saying. "Twice in one day?" he said. "She got hurt twice today? Twice before the dance tryout? And you were there both times?"

"Y-yes," I said. "But I never touched her. That's the truth."

He stared hard at me.

"You believe me—don't you?" I demanded. "Don't you?"

He lowered his eyes. "Of course," he said. "I believe you."

But something in his voice had changed. He wasn't looking at me. He suddenly seemed nervous.

He doesn't believe me, I realized.

He thinks that Jilly getting hurt twice in one day is too big a coincidence.

But it was a coincidence. I know it was.

A cold blast of wind made the trees shift and creak. Leaves showered down all around us. I shivered, suddenly feeling cold, so cold all over.

"Jilly is my good friend," I said. "I would never hurt her. No way."

"Of course not," Glen said. But he still avoided my eyes.

"I—I've got to get home," I said. I took off, running hard. "Later."

"Later," he called after me.

I ran about half a block and stopped at the corner. When I turned around, I saw that Glen hadn't moved. He was still standing there in front of the school, hands shoved in his pockets, watching me, staring hard at me.

And even from so far away, I could see the unhappy, troubled look on his face.

I didn't go home. I went to Jilly's house instead.

I knew that Jilly's parents were probably on their way to the hospital. But I wanted to tell Jackie and Judy what had happened.

Judy opened the door. Her eyes were red-rimmed.

She looked as if she'd been crying. "What a horrible night. Mom, Dad, and Jackie are on their way to Cedar Bay General," she said in a rush. "Maggie—what happened? Is Jilly going to be okay?"

"Yes," I said, stepping past her into the house. The house smelled of fried onions. I heard the dishwasher chugging away in the kitchen. Judy had her homework spread out all over the living room floor. "Her ankle was really swollen. It's probably broken. But she should be okay."

Judy started pacing the living room tensely. "But what happened? Did she slip or something?"

I sighed. I still felt so cold. I decided to keep my coat on. "It's hard to explain. It was totally weird, Judy. She just started spinning. It wasn't part of the dance or anything. She was spinning and . . . I guess she lost control."

Judy shook her head. "Poor Jilly. She worked so hard for this."

I dropped down heavily into an armchair. "She might have cracked some ribs, too," I added softly.

Judy grabbed her side, as if feeling Jilly's pain. "Wow. I—I should have gone to the hospital. I didn't know it was so bad."

I nodded. I didn't know what else to say.

Should I tell Judy that her sister blamed me for the whole thing? That she accused me of using my evil powers on her?

No, I decided.

Ms. Masters was right. Jilly was in shock. She didn't know what she was saying.

Judy suddenly stopped pacing. Her expression changed. She crossed the room and sat down on the arm of my chair. "Can I ask you something?"

"Yeah. Sure," I said.

Judy's dark eyes locked on mine. "Remember when you were over here yesterday and you were petting Plumper?"

"Of course," I replied. "How could I forget it? I was so shocked. First the cat goes psycho. Then he decides he likes me."

Judy swallowed. She continued to stare at me. "Well, were you wearing any weird kind of lotion or cream or anything on your hands?"

I blinked. "Excuse me?"

"You know. You're always trying new cosmetics, right? So did you have anything on your hands yesterday? Some kind of hand cream?"

"No. No way," I said. I gazed up at Judy, bewildered. "Why?"

Judy frowned. "I'll show you," she said. She slid off the chair arm and disappeared from the room.

A few seconds later she returned carrying Plumper in both arms like a baby. The big cat lay limply in her arms.

I climbed to my feet. I could tell instantly that something was weird. He never let Judy carry him around.

"Did you wash your hands in some new kind of soap?" Judy asked. "Think hard. Did you touch anything strange in chemistry lab yesterday?"

I shook my head. "No way. What is the problem?"

"Look at him," Judy replied, setting Plumper down on the floor.

I let out a gasp when I saw the cat's back. It took me a while to realize that the wide stripe I stared at was yellow-pink-splotched skin. Bare cat skin. Skin where the thick, orange fur had been.

"Look at that," Judy said sadly. "All the fur on his back. It all fell out after you left, Maggie. In big clumps. It just all fell out. Only where you touched him . . ."

I hurried home. The house was dark except for the front hall light.

I found a note from Mom stuck to the fridge. It said that she was called for emergency room duty. She'd be at the hospital all night. The note ended: "Hope you danced up a storm! Love, Mom."

Well . . . there was a storm, all right! I thought bitterly.

Then I realized: If Mom is on emergency room duty, she'll probably see Jilly come in. And she'll get the whole horrible story from Jilly.

Will Jilly blame me in front of my own mother?

With a weary groan I tossed the bag with my ballet slippers onto the kitchen counter. I suddenly realized I was still in my tights and leotard. I pulled open the fridge, grabbed a diet soda, and hurried up to my room to get changed.

I pulled on a long, woolly nightshirt and a pair of heavy, warm white socks. I was standing in front of

83

my dresser mirror, absently running a brush through my hair, thinking . . .

What is going on?

So many strange, horrible things had happened in the past few days. Since my birthday . . . since the fortune-teller read my hand.

Glen's lawn mower out of control. Poor Chirpy. Judy's cat attacking me. Then losing all his fur. And Jilly . . . falling down the stairs at school . . . twirling out of control onstage . . . and accusing me . . . accusing me!

Such an ugly jumble of pictures in my mind.

Was it possible that I was causing these things to happen? Was it possible the fortune-teller had seen the truth about me?

No . . . no . . . no . . .

There's no such thing as evil powers.

I was still gazing into the mirror when the phone rang.

It must be Jackie or Judy to tell me how Jilly is doing, I decided.

My heart started to pound. I had a sudden, heavy feeling of dread in my stomach.

What if she isn't okay?

What if her injuries were worse than everyone thought?

I grabbed the phone, pressed it to my ear, and uttered a tense, "Hello?"

"Hello, Sugar?"

Not the voice I expected to hear. Through heavy static, I recognized the voice of my dad.

"Sugar? It's me."

I absolutely hate the fact that he always calls me Sugar or some other cutesy name. He never calls me by my name. Sometimes I think it's because he doesn't remember it!

"Hi, Dad."

"Am I calling too late?"

"No. It's only eleven," I said, glancing at my bed table clock. "Where are you?"

"I'm in the car," he replied, shouting over the static. "On the freeway. Not a very good connection." He said something else, but a loud buzz covered it up.

"How's your mother?" he asked when the buzzing stopped.

"Okay," I said. "She's at work."

"Sorry I missed your birthday, Punkin," he said.

It's only the tenth birthday in a row that you've missed! I thought.

But I said, "That's okay."

"Did you—" More static drowned out his question.

"What did you say, Daddy?" I shouted, pressing the phone tighter against my ear. "This horrible connection—"

"Did you get my present?" he repeated.

"No," I said. "Not yet."

I knew he hadn't sent a present. No way. He

didn't even remember to call!

"Keep watching for it," he said, followed by more static. "What's new at school, Sugar? Tell me some news."

I hunched down on the edge of my bed. "Well . . . I had a tryout tonight, and it looks as if I'll be in the new town dance company."

A long pause. "Dance company? Really?" he asked. "I didn't know you were into dance."

Only my whole life!

"Yeah. I'm really into it," I said.

"I'm sorry. This is such a bad connection, Punkin. I'd better say good night."

"I—I'm glad you called," I shouted over the static.

And then—I had to ask.

I don't know why. I knew it was totally crazy. I knew Dad would only think I was weird.

But I had to. I had to ask while I had him on the phone.

I stood up. "Can I ask you a question, and you promise not to laugh at me?" I shouted.

"What?" he replied. "Oh, yeah. Okay. Go ahead."

"Dad . . . Is there something strange about me? Do I have some kind of weird powers?"

A burst of static on the other end. I pressed the phone tighter to my ear.

What did he say? What was his answer?

"I can't talk about it."

Is that what he said?

That couldn't be it—could it?

No. I didn't hear him right.

"Dad? Dad?" I cried. "Are you still there? What did you say?"

Silence.

"Dad? Dad?"

Silence.

The connection was lost.

I stared at the phone. I knew I hadn't heard correctly. I knew I got it wrong.

"I can't talk about it."

No. No way.

What kind of an answer was that?

Before school the next morning I ran into Glen at his locker. "How's it going?" I asked.

"Okay." He slammed the locker door shut.

I shifted my backpack on my shoulder. "Where are you headed? What's your first class?"

He glanced nervously from side to side, as if searching for someone else to talk to. "Music Appreciation," he said. "Hey, I gotta go." He hoisted his backpack up by the straps with one hand and hurried away.

He was so unfriendly.

He seemed afraid of me, I realized.

Across the hall I saw Deena and Marci staring at me. They looked away when I waved to them. But I made my way over to them.

"Hey—hi!"

I was still thinking about how unfriendly Glen had been. But I tried to sound cheerful. "I like your vest," I told Marci. "Cool color."

Marci didn't reply. She glanced at Deena.

"Did you hear anything about Jilly?" Deena asked.

"Not yet," I said. I gazed down the hall. "I'll ask one of her sisters when they get here."

They both nodded coldly. Then they turned and started to walk away.

"That was so horrible last night," I called after them.

Marci spun around to face me. Her pale cheeks reddened. Her eyes burned into mine. "Why did Jilly say that stuff about you last night, Maggie?"

I swallowed. "Excuse me?"

"Why did Jilly blame you for what happened? Why did she say you were evil?"

"I don't know!" I cried shrilly. "I don't know why she said that! I really don't! You've got to believe me!"

They both just stared at me. As if I were some kind of lab specimen or strange creature from another planet.

They didn't say another word. They turned and hurried away.

I stood there in the middle of the hall, breathing hard, my heart racing. I felt so bad. I could feel hot tears on my cheeks.

Did Marci and Deena believe what Jilly said?

Did Glen think I did something to Jilly so that I'd make the dance company?

How could they think such a crazy, horrible thing?

When I spotted Jackie striding down the hall, I was so happy to see a friendly face. I wanted to grab her and hug her.

Wiping the tears away with both hands, I ran toward her. "Jackie—hi! How is Jilly?" I called.

She shrugged. "I guess she's okay," she said. "I mean, it could have been a lot worse."

"What did the doctors say?" I asked breathlessly.

Jackie sighed. "Well . . . she has a badly sprained ankle. And two bruised ribs."

"Oh, wow. Is she . . . is she home?" I asked.

Jackie shook her head, her long, black hair tumbling out from beneath her purple down coat. "Not yet. The doctors want to keep an eye on her a little while longer. They said maybe this afternoon."

She unzipped the coat and crossed the hall to her locker. "It's just so weird," she said. "How could she spin out of control like that? It's crazy!"

"I—I want to see her," I stammered.

Jackie had opened the locker. She was kneeling to pull some books from the bottom. But she turned and gazed up at me. "Not a good idea," she said, frowning.

I opened my mouth to say something, but the words caught in my throat.

"She blames you," Jackie said, standing up. "She thinks you cast a spell on her or something. To make her spin out of control."

"But that's totally insane!" I screamed.

A group of kids turned to stare at me.

"Of course it is," Jackie said. She sighed again. "But Jilly keeps talking about that fortune-teller at the carnival. She keeps saying the fortune-teller wasn't joking. The fortune-teller told the truth. Jilly says what happened to her last night proves it."

"But—but—" I sputtered.

"The doctors tried to explain to Jilly," Jackie continued. "They tried to tell her she probably got carried away last night by the excitement of the dance tryout. She wanted to show everyone what a great dancer she is, and she just lost control."

"Yes. That explains it," I said in a whisper. My throat suddenly felt so tight and dry.

"But Jilly isn't buying it," Jackie said. "Jilly says she could feel a force—a really strong force—making her spin. She says she tried desperately to stop. But she couldn't. She couldn't stop no matter what she did! Something was forcing her to spin!"

I grabbed Jackie's shoulder. "You don't believe that—do you?"

Jackie shook her head. "I don't know what to believe," she muttered. She raised her eyes sadly to me. "I guess I should tell you. There's more."

"Huh? More?" I realized I was holding my breath.

"Judy isn't in school," she said softly. "She and Mom had to take Plumper to the animal hospital this morning."

"Oh, no," I whispered.

"The cat lost his fur. On his back. Where Judy says you petted him. And now he's getting big red and purple sores all over his back."

"No . . ." I repeated. I grabbed Jackie's arm. "You don't believe that's my fault, too—do you? I mean, Judy doesn't blame me for that. She can't. She can't!"

Jackie started to reply. But the bell rang. It was right above our heads, and the jarring electronic buzz made me jump a mile.

Jackie closed her locker and clicked the lock. "Gotta run," she said. "I'm sorry about all this, Maggie. But—"

"Can I come over after school?" I asked desperately. "You and I could study together. Or just talk. Or—"

"Not a good idea right now," she replied. "Maybe I should come to your house instead."

So after school Jackie and I walked to my house together.

We talked about our classes. And our teachers. And a movie Jackie had seen. And about guys in our class.

We talked about everything except Judy and Jilly. I think we both wanted to pretend that none of the bad, frightening stuff from the last week had happened.

In the kitchen I grabbed a bag of pretzels, a couple of apples, and some cans of Sprite. And Jackie and I made our way up to my room.

"I need to see your government notes," I told her. "I know we're supposed to write down everything Mr. McCally says. But I can't listen to him. He puts me right to sleep."

"I think I have the notes with me," Jackie said. "But—first things first." Her eyes lit up as she crossed the room to my dresser and began going through my cosmetics collection. "You're so lucky, Maggie," she said. "Mom won't let us have any of this stuff."

I tore open the pretzel bag and pulled out a handful. "The new stuff is in the top drawer," I told her.

"Yesss!" Jackie cried happily.

She pulled open the top dresser drawer. Began to paw inside. And then I saw her expression change.

Her smile faded. Her eyes bulged.

She gripped the sides of the drawer with both hands.

And opened her mouth in a horrified scream.

"Jackie—! What is it? What is it?" I shrieked.

Jackie let out another high scream.

Her face distorted—in horror, in shock—she reached into the drawer.

"Jackie—?" I cried.

I heard a clattering sound.

She lifted something from the drawer and spun around to show it to me. Raising it in front of her, shaking it, her face wild with fury.

Her beaded necklace!

"You did take it!" she shrieked. "You're a liar, Maggie! You are evil!"

I stared at the shiny beads, glittering, trembling in her raised hand. A wave of nausea rolled over me.

I felt sick. So sick.

"Jackie—listen to me!" I shrieked. "I don't know how that got there. You've got to listen to me!"

I dived across the room.

But she dodged to the side, angrily scooting away from me.

Gripping the necklace tightly in one hand, she

raised her other hand and pointed at me. "Evil," she muttered. "Evil."

My hands burned again. And my arms tingled.

I stared in horror at Jackie's finger, jerking in the air, pointing, accusing me.

And as I stared, Jackie's finger suddenly tilted up. Up—and then back.

"Hey—!" Jackie let out a startled cry as the finger bent back . . . back . . . back . . .

"Stop it, Maggie!" she pleaded. "It hurts! Stop it!" Back . . . back . . .

And then the finger snapped.

The finger made a sick snapping sound. The sound of cracking bone.

Jackie was screaming now, her eyes bulging, her mouth gaping in howls of pain.

I screamed too, pressing my burning hands against the sides of my face.

The crack of her finger repeated in my ears, again and again.

And then, holding her hand high, Jackie lurched out into the hall. She went flying down the stairs, hurtling them two at a time.

"Please! Listen to me!" I pleaded.

She jerked open the front door. She didn't turn around. She leaped off the front stoop and ran full speed down our gravel driveway. Gravel flew under her shoes.

"Jackie—stop!" I screamed.

She let out a cry as she fell. Stumbled on the stones of the driveway and sprawled face forward. She landed hard on her knees and elbows. Her backpack thudded away from her.

"Jackie—" I ran after her.

But she was on her feet. Hair flying wildly around her flaming red face.

"Jackie—come back!" I begged.

But she scooped up her backpack with her good hand. Then, trembling, she turned furiously to me. "Leave us alone, Maggie!" she shrieked. "Leave my family alone! You've done enough! Just leave us alone!"

I slumped to the ground. I buried my face in my hands. My whole body was shaking.

I took a deep breath and struggled to stop the powerful shudders. When I uncovered my face, Jackie was gone.

For a moment I thought it had all been a bad dream. Some kind of frightening nightmare.

I'm going to wake up in bed, I thought. And none of this will have happened.

But no. Here I was on the front stoop. The front door wide open behind me. Awake. Wide awake.

I climbed to my feet and made my way back up to my room. The top dresser drawer stood open. I slammed it shut with an angry cry. Then I threw myself down on my bed and buried my head in the pillow.

How did that necklace get in there? I asked myself. How?

Why did Jackie's finger snap back like that?

Why are these things happening?

Jilly was back in school on Friday. She walked on crutches. She had a cast on her foot.

She wouldn't talk to me.

Jackie wouldn't talk to me, either. She and Jilly turned their backs whenever I came near.

I felt so upset, I could barely speak.

"Give them time," Judy told me. "They're totally upset now. But they'll come around, Maggie. They'll realize there's no such thing as evil powers." She squeezed my arm. "I'm still your friend. And I know you would never do anything to hurt us."

Judy cheered me up a little. But word about my so-called evil got around school quickly.

In the lunchroom at noon kids were staring at me. I passed a table of laughing girls—and they all stopped laughing when I came near.

Carrying my lunch tray, I searched for an empty seat. The whole lunchroom grew quiet. An unnatural hush.

Everyone stared at me. Everyone hoped I wouldn't sit next to them.

I tried to talk to some guys I always kid around with. But they ignored me and leaned across the table to talk to each other.

They're all shutting me out, I realized to my horror.

They're all afraid of me. They all believe the rumors. That I'm weird. That I have powers. That I'm evil.

Overnight I've become an outcast. A freak.

I sat down by myself in the far corner and set down my food tray. Kids kept glancing at me, then quickly looked away.

Near the front I saw the Three J's at a table with a couple of guys. Jilly's crutches were propped against the side of the table. She sat at the end so that she could stretch out the leg in a cast.

Jackie said something, and everyone else at the table laughed. Then Jackie and Judy started arguing about something, a playful argument. More laughter.

None of them looked my way.

I couldn't touch my food. My stomach felt hard and tight, like a solid rock. It took all my strength to keep from breaking down and crying my eyes out.

I can't just sit here by myself for the rest of the school year, I told myself.

I can't let everyone in school think I'm some kind of evil freak.

I know I'm not evil. I know I have no strange powers of any kind. No powers at all.

Now I have to prove it to my friends. I have to prove to my friends that I'm just me, just the same normal me they've always known.

But how? How can I prove it to them?

I stared at the three sisters across the room, laughing and enjoying their lunch. I stared hard at them, thinking . . . thinking . . .

And suddenly I had an idea.

I left my food behind, took a deep breath, and crossing my arms tightly in front of me, I walked over to the three sisters' table. "I want to talk to you," I said. My voice came out tight and tense, almost like a growl.

Jackie swallowed a bite of her sandwich, then stared down at the cast on her hand. "Maggie, please go away," she said softly.

"No," I insisted. "I want to show you something."

Jilly stared at her food. Jackie scowled at me. "I asked you nicely," she said. "Please don't bother us."

"I—I'm going to prove that you're wrong about me," I said, wrapping my arms around myself tighter to stop my trembling. "We've been friends for a long time. You owe it to me. Just give me two minutes to prove to you that you're wrong."

Jackie kept scowling, her face growing redder and redder. But I stared her down.

"Two minutes?" she said finally.

I nodded. "Yes. Two minutes. I'm going to prove

to all of you that I have no powers. That fortune-teller was crazy. I'm totally normal. I'm not a witch, and I'm going to prove it."

"Give her a chance," Judy said. "Come on. Give her a chance."

"Can I sit down?" I asked.

Jackie nodded. "Go ahead. Two minutes. We'll give you two minutes. Then do you promise you won't do any more horrible things to me and my sisters?"

I pulled out the chair and slid into it. "I haven't done anything to you," I said.

"How are you going to prove it?" Judy asked.

I turned to watch the lunch line. I saw Marci pick up her food tray and carry it to the cash register to pay.

"See Marci over there?" I asked, pointing.

The three sisters turned their heads to look at her.

"I'm going to concentrate on her as hard as I can," I told them. "I'll try to make her stumble and drop her lunch tray. I'll concentrate all my powers. And you'll see. Nothing will happen."

Jilly laughed. "That's so stupid!" she sneered.

Jackie shook her head. "We're not idiots, Maggie. We know what you'll do. You'll only pretend to concentrate. You can make Marci trip if you want to—but you won't do it. You'll pretend. You'll fake the whole thing."

"Anyone can say they're concentrating when

they're not," Jilly added. "It's no kind of test at all."

"But I promise!" I said. I placed my hand over my heart. "I swear it! I swear I'll concentrate as hard as I can to make Marci trip. Believe me. Please— believe me. There she goes. Watch. She won't trip. She won't—because I have no powers."

Balancing the tray in both hands, Marci moved away from the cash register. She gazed around the crowded room, looking for a friend to sit with.

I narrowed my eyes on her. Concentrated . . . concentrated all my energy. And my hands started to burn. I felt tingling up and down my arms. And my hands . . . my hands felt as if they were on fire.

It's happening again, I realized. Is it some kind of power? Some kind of force flowing through me—a force so powerful it burns?

My hands smoldered as if I were holding them on a stove burner. The pain throbbed up my arms.

I turned away from Marci. Don't look at her, I thought. If you don't look at her, nothing bad will happen.

I grabbed a cold can of soda from the table. I gripped it tightly, wrapped my burning hands around it, trying to cool them off.

But my hands grew hotter.

I stared hard at the soda, willing my hands to cool down.

I stared at the soda so I wouldn't look at Marci.

But my eyes lifted. They bored into Marci. No!

No! I thought. Don't look at her!

I tried to turn away, but I couldn't.

I tried to shut my eyes, but they wouldn't close.

Marci took three steps toward the tables—and stumbled over her own feet.

She let out a startled cry—and her tray went flying.

She fell and landed hard on her stomach. The tray clattered to the floor beside her, plates bouncing, food spilling, her apple juice overturned, puddling over the floor.

I uttered a horrified cry. Turned to see Jilly and Jackie glaring at me, their faces twisted in shock, in fear.

Before I could say anything, I heard another loud cry from the back of the lunchroom. I turned in time to see a boy crossing the room with a tray. His hands flew up, and he tumbled to the floor. His tray fell, bounced once on the edge of a table, and crashed to the floor.

Some kids laughed and cheered. But the room was mostly silent now.

Am I doing this? I wondered, staring at my burning hot hands.

If I am, I've got to stop it. I've got to concentrate on stopping it.

Stop! I thought. Stop! I concentrated hard, repeating the word over and over in my mind. Stop! Stop!

In front of the cash register, Cindy, a girl from one

of my classes, stumbled and fell—and her food tray flew out of her hands, sailed high, and came down on her head.

Two girls fell off their chairs. The chairs toppled over on top of them.

More laughter. But I heard startled gasps, and a few kids were screaming.

Stop! I thought, concentrating hard. Stop this—now!

I let the soda drop to the floor.

I pressed my hands against my ears as another tray crashed. A girl in the food line fell into a plate of spaghetti.

I heard a loud groan. A boy jumped up from his chair, leaned over the table—and let out another hoarse groan, opened his mouth, and vomited his lunch onto the table.

Screams and cries now.

I turned and saw Jilly screaming: "Maggie—stop it! Stop it!"

"Please—stop it!" Jackie was shrieking, too.

Trays crashed. Food splattered over the tables, over the floor. A girl waved her hands wildly above her head. Then she jumped up and began to puke, groaning and heaving.

Two more kids jumped up and started to vomit. Another lunch tray went sliding over the floor. Large platters of food sailed off the counter, soared into the air, and crashed against the wall, sending their contents splashing over the lunchroom.

I saw a girl covered in tomato sauce. Kids were falling, screaming, running for the door. A boy leaned on our table. His eyes rolled back in his head, and he puked his lunch into Jilly's lap.

"Nooooo," I moaned. "This isn't happening. It isn't . . ."

"Maggie did this!" Jackie screamed.

She jumped onto the table. She cupped her hands around her mouth and bellowed at the top of her lungs, "Maggie did this! Maggie did it!"

Kids stampeded to the doors. Others turned to stare at me.

"She's evil!" Jackie screamed, standing on the table, frantically pointing down at me. "Maggie is evil! Maggie did it!"

I covered my ears, trying to force out the shrieks and groans and cries of horror. And I ran, ran out of the lunchroom, and tore through the deserted hall.

"Maggie! Stop!" a voice called.

I spun around. "Glen—!" I cried.

His eyes locked on mine. "Let's get out of here," he said softly. "Some kids and teachers are coming after you."

I gasped. "You—you're helping me?"

He didn't answer. He pushed the door open and guided me outside. "Come on. Run," he whispered.

I heard the thud of rapid footsteps behind us in the hall. I didn't turn around to see who was coming.

I lowered my head and started to run, following Glen across the playground. It was a gray, windy afternoon. Heavy, low clouds made it seem nearly as dark as night. Our shoes crunched over dead leaves as we ran.

I heard shouts from the school behind us. Glen and I crossed the street and kept running.

We didn't stop until we were two blocks away and the school building was no longer in sight. I dropped onto the grass of someone's front lawn, gasping for air, waiting for the pain in my side to fade.

Glen lowered himself beside me. His face was bright red. His hair was so wild about his head, he looked as if he'd been in a hurricane!

"I was in the lunchroom," he said, swallowing. "It . . . was so weird."

I nodded, still struggling to catch my breath.

"Kids said it was your fault," Glen continued, his eyes searching mine. "They said you have evil powers or something."

I snickered bitterly. "Do you believe them? Aren't you afraid of me?"

He swallowed again and brushed back his hair with one hand. "Yeah. I guess I am. A little." He lowered his eyes. "But I saw you needed help. So . . ."

I reached out and squeezed his hand. "Thanks for sticking with me," I whispered.

He looked embarrassed. He pulled his hand away quickly. "What happened back there, Maggie?"

I shook my head unhappily. "I—I don't really know. I don't know if it was my fault or not. I wanted to show Jilly and Jackie that they were wrong about me. But then . . ." My voice trailed off.

My brain was doing flip-flops. I felt dizzy. And so confused.

Glen was still studying me intently. "Do you really have powers?"

"I—I don't know!" I screamed. I didn't mean to scream. It just burst out of me. I jumped to my feet. "I don't know! Stop asking me questions!"

My head felt about to explode. I spun away from Glen and took off.

I saw the startled expression on his face. But I didn't care. I couldn't explain to him what had just happened in the lunchroom. I couldn't explain it to myself!

I had to get away from him, too. I had to go somewhere and think.

I couldn't go back to school. At least, not until things calmed down. And I couldn't go home. Mom would probably be there—and how could I explain?

So I kept running . . . running in a daze. Ignoring the ache in my side from running so hard. Ignoring the pictures of horror from the lunchroom that played over and over in my mind.

A loud wail of a car horn snapped me from a daze. I heard the squeal of brakes and saw the red car swerve—and realized I had run into the street without even looking.

"Are you crazy?" The young man in the driver's seat swung a fist out the window at me. "Want to get killed?"

"Sorry," I called as he roared away.

I shut my eyes. Close call, I thought.

But somehow the shock of the close call had calmed me down. I had stopped trembling. My heart no longer thudded against my chest.

Where am I? I wondered.

The heavy clouds seemed to lower over me. Squinting into the darkening light, I saw that I was only a block from the Cedar Bay Mall.

In the middle of the afternoon the mall would be a safe place to sit down and think, I told myself. Everyone I knew was in school. I didn't have to worry about running into anyone there.

I'll find a quiet place to sit down, and I'll try to figure this all out, I decided.

I'll try to figure out a way to talk to Mom about what happened. I'll force her to tell me the truth about myself.

Mom lied before. I know she did.

I can't kid myself anymore. I have to admit to myself that I do have powers. I've been denying it, denying it, denying it.

But after the scene in the lunchroom, I know better.

I caused those people to trip, those lunch trays to fly. I caused those kids to be sick. My evil thoughts caused it all. I can't deny it any longer.

What am I going to do? I wondered, feeling my panic start to return. I couldn't stop what was happening. I tried to stop it—but it was out of control.

How will I have a normal life? How will I ever have any friends?

I waited for the traffic to clear, then crossed the street and made my way through the parking lot to a mall entrance. Inside, I gazed down the long aisle. The mall was practically empty. A mother pushed her sleeping baby past me in a stroller. An elderly couple, both leaning on bright blue canes, peered into the window of a shoe store.

I passed by a Gap, an Urban Outfitters, a CD store, and a bookstore. Somehow, the blur of bright lights and colors and the bouncy, brassy music from the loudspeakers was comforting.

Normal life. Everything so clean and bright . . . and normal.

I suddenly pictured Glen, the startled look on his face when I took off and ran away from him.

I'll have to apologize later, I decided. That wasn't nice of me at all. He was only trying to help me. He was the only one who wanted to help me.

I took an escalator down one flight. My stomach growled. I remembered that I hadn't eaten any lunch.

I'll grab something to eat at the food court, I decided. Then I'll find a place in a corner where I can sit and think.

I rode down to the lower level. Turned down the aisle that led to the food court—and stopped.

"Oh." I stared hard at the woman in the brightly colored flowered dress coming toward me. I recognized her instantly—and to my shock, she recognized me.

Miss Elizabeth. The fortune-teller.

Her dark eyes bulged. She dropped her shopping bags. Then she scooped them up quickly. Turned. And, long black hair bouncing behind her, started to hurry away.

"No, wait! Please!" I cried, running after her. "Please—wait!"

Miss Elizabeth dropped a shopping bag again. She stopped to pick it up, and I caught up with her.

"Please—" I said.

"I remember you," the fortune-teller said, her eyes studying me coldly.

I stepped in front of her so she couldn't run away. "Tell me the truth," I pleaded. "That night . . . at the carnival . . ."

"I sensed the evil," she said. "I saw it."

"But how can that be?" I asked. "My whole life, I—"

"I can sense it now," Miss Elizabeth interrupted. "The evil you carry. It's so strong."

"I—I just don't understand!" I cried. "I never used to be evil. Up until my birthday I never had any powers!"

The woman stared at me coldly. I caught the fear in her eyes. Her bottom lip trembled. "Let me go now," she said.

"No, wait. Please." I blocked her path. I held up

my hand. "Look at it again. Just look at it. Maybe . . . maybe you made a mistake."

She shook her head. "No. I must go." She raised the shopping bags in her hands. "I have been shopping a long time. My family is waiting."

I shoved my hand into her face. "It will only take a second," I said. "Please—look at my hand. You were wrong the first time. I know you were."

Miss Elizabeth sighed and set down her bags. She reached for my hand and turned it so that the palm was up.

She raised my palm to her face and squinted at it for a second or two.

And then she opened her mouth in a shrill cry—and tossed my hand away as if it were burning hot!

"The evil!" she cried. "It's there on your hand! I made no mistake. It came with your birthday! Thirteen is a powerful number!"

She took a step back, her eyes wide and frightened.

"Wait," I pleaded. "Are you sure—?" I stuck out my hand again.

"Please—don't hurt me!" the woman begged. "Don't hurt me! I have a family. They are waiting."

"I . . . I won't hurt you," I whispered. "I'm . . . sorry." I lowered my hand—my evil hand—to my side. And turned away from the poor, trembling woman.

She grabbed up her bags and scurried away. I

watched her as she rode up the escalator, staring down at me, clutching her bags tightly in front of her as if shielding herself from my evil magic.

At home I shut myself up in my room and didn't even come out for dinner. Mom kept banging on my door, asking what was wrong. "Are you sick? I'm a nurse, remember? Let me look at you."

"No. I just want to be left alone," I called out.

I felt relieved when she left to work the night shift at the hospital. I sat down at my desk and grabbed the telephone.

I'd been thinking hard, thinking for hours.

At first my thoughts were filled with anger. Anger and despair.

My life is over, I thought. I'm doomed—doomed to a horrible, lonely life.

A life without friends. With everyone hating me, terrified of me.

But then I started thinking about my powers. I have powers, I knew. I definitely have powers. But do they have to be evil?

I thought about those old TV shows they run on Nickelodeon all the time at night. The one with the genie who is always popping in and out, doing cute magic. And the other show—*Bewitched*—with the cute, blond witch.

Everyone thinks they're funny, I told myself. No one hates them. Everyone thinks they're terrific!

I knew they were only TV sitcoms. There wasn't anything real about them. But they started me thinking in a whole new way.

They gave me a little bit of hope.

So I sat down at my desk and phoned Jackie.

At first she didn't want to talk to me. "Haven't you caused enough damage?" she asked angrily. "What more do you want, Maggie?"

"I want my friends," I said. "I want you and your sisters not to hate me. I don't want everyone in school to stare at me like I'm some kind of freak, and hide from me, and think I'm evil."

"But—but you are evil!" Jackie sputtered. "You proved it—in the lunchroom. Even Judy had to admit it."

"No—!" I protested. "Listen to me, Jackie. Please don't hang up. Give me a chance."

"I've got to study," she replied. "I can't spend time on the phone. I have that algebra test first thing tomorrow morning, and you know it's my worst subject."

"I have the test, too," I said. "Listen, I've been thinking . . ."

"I've got to go, Maggie. Really—"

"Maybe I do have powers," I continued. "In fact, yes. Okay—yes. I do have powers. I don't know how. I don't know why. But I seem to have them."

"Maggie, you've already hurt my family so much!" Jackie declared.

"Well—what if I use my powers for good?" I asked. "If I can do evil things, I can do good things, too—right?"

"I don't know," Jackie said impatiently. "The whole thing is too creepy, too yucky. Everyone is scared of you now, Maggie, and—and so am I."

"But what if I do something good tomorrow? What if I use my powers to get you an A on the algebra test?"

Jackie uttered a startled cry. "Excuse me?"

"I'll get you an A tomorrow," I repeated. "I'll concentrate all my powers. I promise. I'll—"

"Concentrate your powers? Like in the lunchroom?" she interrupted.

"I'll concentrate all my powers and get you an A on the test," I said.

"Well . . ."

"I want you to stay my friend," I told her. "I'll do it for you. Really. You'll see. And if I do it, you have to promise not to hate me."

Again, she hesitated. "Well . . . we'll see, Maggie. See you tomorrow." And she hung up.

I sat at the desk, gripping the phone, staring out the window at the black night sky.

I just made a big promise. Can I do it? I wondered.

Can I?

The next morning I met Jackie outside the algebra classroom. I ignored the kids staring at me up and down the hall. I saw them whispering as I passed. And I saw several kids back away, as if I carried a disease or something they might catch.

"Ready?" I asked her.

She eyed me intently, as if she'd never seen me before. "I'm sorry," she said. "I—I don't know what to think. You've done so much harm. Poor Jilly had to stay home today. Her ribs hurt too bad. She could barely get out of bed."

I lowered my eyes. "I'm really sorry," I muttered. "I didn't mean to hurt Jilly or you. You've got to believe me. It was before I realized—"

"Let's just go in," Jackie said sharply. "Kids are looking at us." She started into the classroom.

"I'm going to do what I promised," I whispered as I followed her in. "I'm going to concentrate all my powers. You'll see. I can do good, too."

We took our seats. Jackie sat in the same row as me, two seats away.

When I sat down, Cory Hassell, the boy who sits next to me, scooted his desk as far from mine as he could. Then he leaned over to me and whispered, "Are you going to make everyone puke their guts out today?"

I rolled my eyes. "Give me a break, Cory. That was not my fault yesterday. I don't know how these dumb rumors start—do you?"

He didn't answer. He sat back up and pretended to study his algebra textbook.

The bell rang. Mrs. Rodgers got everyone quiet. Then she walked up and down the aisles, passing out the tests.

She stopped when she got to my desk, and peered down at me. "How are you feeling today, Maggie?" she asked.

"Fine," I replied. I took the test from her.

She stared at me for a few seconds more. She looked as if she wanted to ask me another question. But she didn't. She moved on down the row.

"Everyone begin," she instructed when she had returned to her desk. "It's a difficult exam. But you should have enough time to complete it."

A heavy silence fell over the room. I glanced around at all the heads bowed low over the test questions. Pencils scratched. One girl was already erasing violently.

Did she get her name wrong? I wondered.

I shut my eyes and started to concentrate.

I concentrated on Jackie. I pictured her in my mind, filling out the test, getting all the answers right.

Jackie will get a perfect score, I told myself.

I was catching on to how these powers worked. I just had to concentrate on something—and it came true.

So I lowered my head and shut my eyes, and wished for Jackie to get a perfect score on the algebra test. Wished . . . concentrated hard . . .

And yes. Once again, the skin on my arms started to prickle. My hands burned . . . burned so hot . . .

My eyes snapped open when I heard a sharp cry. I recognized the voice. Jackie!

I turned down the row—in time to see Jackie leap up from her seat. "Oh! Oh, nooo!" she wailed.

Bright red blood poured from her nose.

The blood splashed onto her test paper. It ran down the front of her yellow T-shirt.

Mrs. Rodgers looked up from her desk. "Oh, what a bad nosebleed!" she declared.

The blood flowed from both of Jackie's nostrils. Two rivers of gleaming, scarlet blood.

Jackie jammed her hand over her nose. But it didn't stop the nosebleed. In seconds the blood flowed over the side of her hand.

Mrs. Rodgers ran up beside Jackie and took her by the elbow. "Quick—go to the nurse! She'll know how to stop it. Hurry, Jackie! Oh, my. I've never seen so much blood!"

Jackie staggered to the door, cupping her hand over her nose, leaving a bright trail of blood on the floor.

"I'd better go with you," Mrs. Rodgers said. "Just keep doing your tests, everyone. And no talking." She hurried after Jackie.

Jackie stopped at the classroom door. She turned and pointed at me. "Evil!" she cried.

One word.

That's all.

Evil.

Then she and the teacher disappeared out the door.

"Whoa. That was so gross!" someone said.

"Poor Jackie."

Then the classroom returned to silence. I lowered my head and shut my eyes again. I was trembling so hard, I gripped the sides of my chair to steady myself.

My breath caught in my throat. My chest ached.

Evil. I can only do evil, I realized.

I wanted to help Jackie. I tried to help her. But my powers can be used only for evil.

And I can't control them. I do these horrible, evil things to my friends because I have no control over my powers!

Then, behind me, I thought I heard a boy begin to chant—softly at first, and then louder.

And then some girls joined in. Then more voices. More voices chanting.

And as I sat there trembling, sick, terrified, it sounded as if the entire class chanted, slowly, in a slow, steady rhythm, softly, so softly, like distant thunder.

All of them.

All of them, leaning over their test papers, chanting: "EVIL . . . EVIL . . . EVIL . . . EVIL . . . EVIL . . . EVIL . . . EVIL . . ."

After dinner that night I rode my bike over to Glen's house.

I didn't know where else to go. Who else could I talk to?

He seemed really surprised to see me. He led me into a tiny den beside the living room. It looked like some kind of hunting lodge from an old movie. The walls were covered with huge art posters of tigers and elephants. The chairs and couch were all beat up, cracked, dark brown leather. A long hunting rifle was mounted over the doorway.

"I don't know what to do," I said. "I thought maybe you—"

What did I think? Why was I there?

I suddenly felt very confused.

Glen motioned for me to sit down in one of the broken leather chairs. "I heard about Jackie," he said, dropping into the chair across from me.

"And did you hear . . ." I started. But it was hard to force the words out. "Did you hear that everyone blames me?"

He nodded. "It's crazy," he murmured, lowering his eyes to the floor. "I keep hearing rumors about you, Maggie. Kids are talking. You know. After that thing in the lunchroom . . ." His voice trailed off.

I sprang up from the chair. "What am I going to do now?" I wailed.

He shook his head. "I don't know what to say. It's so . . . scary." He narrowed his eyes at me. "You're not going to do something evil to me—are you?"

I let out a sigh. "Of course I'm not. But . . . that's the scariest part. Don't you see, Glen? I don't know why these evil things are happening. And I can't control them when they do happen!"

He continued to stare hard at me.

"I don't mean to hurt anyone!" I cried. "How can I prove that to everyone? How can I stop everyone at school from thinking I'm some kind of evil witch?"

Glen shrugged. "I don't know. Maybe . . . maybe if you showed kids you were normal . . . If you showed them that bad things don't always happen when you're there . . . After a while, kids would forget about the rumors."

I bit my bottom lip. "Yes, that's true. But—"

"I know!" He jumped to his feet. "How about the Pet Fair tomorrow morning?"

"Huh? What about it?"

"It's at the Community Center. Just about everyone from school will be there, Maggie. If you show up and help out—"

"I was supposed to help out," I interrupted. "Judy wanted me to help her, but—"

"Great!" Glen cried excitedly. "If you help out at the Pet Fair, and nothing bad happens, kids will start to see that you're not evil. That you're totally normal."

I hesitated. "Well . . ."

"Do it!" Glen urged. He grabbed my hand and squeezed it. "Do it, Maggie. It's worth a try! Do it! What can you lose?"

The Community Center is a long, red brick building with a gym and an auditorium, built beside the Cedar Bay public swimming pool. It's used mainly for town suppers and parties. Kids don't hang out there, but sometimes my friends and I like to explore the thick woods that stretch behind the building for miles.

I woke up early Saturday morning. Pulled on a clean pair of khakis and a sweatshirt. Grabbed a glass of orange juice and an untoasted Pop-Tart for breakfast. And rode my bike through the chilly morning fog, across town to the Pet Fair.

My plan was to get there early so that I could help Judy set up. But as I parked my bike in the rack at the side of the building, I heard cat yowls and barking dogs from inside.

I stepped inside and saw that the big, brightly lit gym was already filled with kids and their pets. As I waited for my eyes to adjust to the bright light, I glimpsed cats in cages and boxes, hamsters, ferrets, and dogs of all sizes and colors. A boy from my class had a fat, green-and-yellow snake curled around his wrist.

Most of the animals didn't seem happy to be there. They were all yowling and howling. Kids were shouting and laughing and showing off their pets. At the front of the gym some blue-uniformed workers were setting up a podium and microphone.

I searched for Judy and finally found her at the far side of the room. She was scurrying around from one group of kids to the other. "All cats against this wall!" she shouted, motioning to the front wall. "Please—try to keep your pet with you!"

"When is the judging?" a girl shouted to Judy.

Judy's answer was drowned out by two dogs growling fiercely at each other.

"Please! Keep your pets calm!" Judy shouted. "All cats over here! Dogs against that wall!"

At the front a man started to test the microphone. It let out a deafening, shrill whistle. That made all the dogs go crazy—howling, barking, straining to pull free of their leashes.

Judy definitely needs my help! I told myself.

I started to make my way to her through the pets and pet cages. But I stopped when I saw a cat I recognized.

Plumper!

Somehow, Plumper must have escaped from his carrier. The cat was slinking low across the gym. His yellow eyes were locked on a cage on the floor, a cage filled with white mice!

I saw Plumper's back arch as he prepared to attack the mice.

"Plumper—no!" I cried. I swooped down on him and lifted him into my arms.

Plumper screeched his unhappiness. He swiped a paw at me, but I held him away from my body. He couldn't reach me.

"Judy—!" I called, running to her, the squirming cat in my arms. "Plumper got free! He—"

Judy spun around at the sound of my voice.

"Here. Here's your cat," I said breathlessly. I reached Plumper out to her. "I—I came to help out."

To my surprise, Judy let out an angry shriek. She grabbed Plumper from me. "Give me that cat!" she screamed. "Don't touch my cat! Get out! Get out of here! We don't want you here!"

Trembling, I backed away.

I saw kids looking at me.

The gym grew quiet.

"Get out! Get out!" Judy screeched at the top of her lungs. "You're evil! Get out!"

"N-no—!" I cried. "Please—don't do this!"

Everyone was staring at me in silence now. Even the animals were quiet.

"You're evil, Maggie!" Judy shrieked. She raised Plumper out toward me as if preparing the cat to attack me. "We don't want you here! Get out! Out!"

My legs were trembling so hard, I could barely move. Somehow I backed to the gym door. My breath came in loud sobs.

So many eyes staring at me. All the kids . . . all the kids I knew . . . staring at me so coldly . . . with so much fear . . . so afraid of me.

They all hate me! I realized. Everyone . . . everyone I know.

It was too much. Too much to bear.

I started to back out the door. And then I stopped. And I pointed to Judy.

"Judy—!" I screamed her name. "Judy—! You shouldn't have done that!"

My arms tingled. Heat soared through my hands. I gasped as a bright red flame shot out of a finger.

I heard an electric crackle. Sparks burst from my hands.

In shock I jerked up both hands—and long, angry flames shot out from all my fingertips.

Screams of fright rang out across the room.

And then the screams were drowned out . . . drowned out by the wails and howls of the animals.

Dogs howled and struggled to tear free of their leashes.

Cats began to hiss. So loud and shrill . . . hissing in rage . . . The most terrifying sound I ever heard . . . like rushing water . . . like air escaping . . . The hiss of evil, of true menace.

And then I stumbled back as the hissing cats

began to claw furiously through their cages and carrying cases.

Across from me a black cat's eyes glowed bright yellow. With an almost human cry it swiped a claw at its owner. Then sank its fangs into her leg.

Screaming in panic, she struggled furiously to kick the cat off.

I turned to see a Dalmatian puppy begin to froth at the mouth. Its eyes spun wildly in its head. It tossed back its head and let out a fierce roar.

"No," I whispered. "Nooooo."

A snake curled itself around a girl's waist, tightening, twisting. The girl screamed, tugging at it helplessly with both hands, red in the face, struggling to breathe.

White mice, squealing, snapping their fat pink tails behind them like whips, stampeded across the floor.

Two wild, snarling dogs attacked each other. Their snapping teeth ripped off huge chunks of fur and skin. Bright red blood puddled beneath them as they battled.

Cats clawed at their owners. Dogs frothed and howled.

Kids scrambled over the floor, wrestling, fighting, frantically struggling to escape their howling, raging pets.

My hand still burned. Flames crackled from my fingertips.

I saw Judy against the back wall. Her hands were raised high as if in surrender. Her mouth was open in an endless scream of horror.

I pointed to her and called. "Judy—! Judy—!"

And to my shock the animals all turned. Turned away from their noisy, angry battles. Broke away from their horrified owners.

The animals all turned. And moved forward as if following orders. They circled Judy. A tight circle of frothing, growling creatures. Chests heaving. Eyes glowing with menace.

They began closing in on her.

Lowering their heads. Arching their backs. Snapping frothy jaws. Drooling hungrily. Preparing to attack.

Closing in. The circle growing tighter . . . tighter.

Judy hunched helplessly in the middle. Trembling. Her entire body shuddering.

They're going to kill her, I realized.

They're moving in for the kill. And it's all my fault. What can I do? What?

Suddenly I knew. I had to leave. If I left the hall, maybe . . . just maybe . . . the animals would return to normal. And Judy would be saved.

So I spun away. Stumbled shakily, dizzily out the door—and started to run.

Out of the building. Back into the cold morning, still foggy and gray.

Past the parking lot and the bike rack. Around the side of the building.

Into the woods. Into the clean, sharp-smelling woods. Into the darkness, the safe darkness under the autumn-bare trees. Twigs and leaves cracking and snapping beneath my shoes.

I followed a twisting, bramble-choked path that curved through the old trees and the low, tangled shrubs. I ran . . . ran blindly . . . ran till I couldn't hear the cries from the building any longer.

And then I stopped just beyond a line of evergreen shrubs. Stopped to catch my breath.

And heard the thud of rapid, approaching footsteps.

The kids in the gym—they're following me! I realized.

They're coming to get me!

With a sharp gasp I ducked low behind the ever-green shrubs. Brambles clung to my sweatshirt sleeves. Wet leaves stuck to my shoes.

I couldn't stop my wheezing breaths.

I struggled to hear the footsteps. Had anyone seen me?

What were they going to do to me when they caught me?

My side ached. My chest felt about to burst.

I peered over the top of the shrub.

"Glen—!" My cry came out in a hoarse whisper. "Glen—it's only you!"

I was so glad to see him. I jumped to my feet, my heart pounding.

His denim jacket flapped around him as he ran. "Are you okay?" he asked, his eyes studying me. "I heard—"

"It was so horrible!" I cried. "I—I'm evil. I—I just did a terrible thing. I can't ever go back. I—I have no friends now. I have no life!"

He raised a finger to his lips. "Sshhhhh. Try to calm down, Maggie."

"How can I?" I shrieked. "I'll never calm down. Never! Don't you understand, Glen? I'm all alone now. A freak! A horrible, evil freak!"

He kept his finger to his lips. "Maggie, I'm still your friend."

"But—but—" I protested.

"It's you and me now," he said softly. "You and me against all of them."

"But my friends," I whispered. "My friends . . . Jackie and Judy and Jilly—"

Glen's expression changed. His eyes grew cold. His whole face tightened. "They deserved it," he rasped. "They deserved everything they got."

I swallowed hard, startled by the change in his voice, the icy expression on his face.

"But, Glen—"

"They're total phonies," he sneered. "Good riddance to them, Maggie. That's what you should be saying. Good riddance."

"No, you're wrong," I protested. "Those girls have been my friends for a long, long time. And—"

"All three of them are so cruel, so cold," Glen continued, ignoring my words. "And they're so totally jealous of you, Maggie. Didn't you see how jealous they were?"

"No," I replied sharply. "That isn't true. They—"

"They've always been jealous of you," Glen

insisted. "I can't believe you're so blind to them. They were never your friends. Never."

He shut his angry eyes for a moment. I saw that he was grinding his teeth, his jaw working back and forth tensely.

When he opened his eyes, he appeared even angrier.

"You should never have trusted those three," he said, shaking his head. "Never. Believe me, they can't be trusted. Know what, Maggie? I'll bet Jackie hid her necklace in your dresser drawer just to make you look bad."

"Huh?" I let out a gasp and staggered back, away from him. A wave of fear swept over me. My whole body trembled.

"Glen—!" I cried. "How—how did you know about Jackie's necklace? I never told you about that!"

Glen stared at me without blinking. "What difference does it make?" he said finally. "It's you and me
now. Us against them."

"But—how did you know about that?" I
repeated.

Dizzying thoughts flashed through my brain.
Glen knew about the necklace in my dresser drawer.
And he was always there . . . always there right after
something horrible happened.

I gasped. I couldn't hold the words back. "It was
you all along—wasn't it!" I whispered. "You—you're
evil!"

To my surprise, Glen tossed back his head and
laughed, a cold, cruel laugh. "Of course it was me!"
he said. "Did you really think you had powers?"

"Y-yes," I answered. "I—I had that strange feeling
each time. My hands burned. Flames shot out. I did
think I had powers."

"No way," Glen said, grinning a sick, ugly grin. "It
was all me. I shared some of my powers with you.

You don't have any powers, Maggie."

And then, the grin fading, he added bitterly, "You're just a normal girl. A normal, average girl. You're not like me."

I stared hard at him, stared hard until he blurred into the dark shrubs and trees.

Suddenly I remembered. I remembered my birthday. The carnival. Before I went in to see the fortune-teller, Glen held my hand. He was goofing around, and he kissed my hand.

The hand the fortune-teller read.

Miss Elizabeth— she saw Glen's evil on my hand! She sensed his evil. Because he held my hand and spread his evil onto me.

And in the mall. When I ran into the fortune-teller in the mall . . . I had squeezed Glen's hand on the way to the mall, just before I saw her.

Miss Elizabeth never saw my evil on my hand. Because both times she was reading Glen's evil!

The sky darkened. The shadows of the trees lengthened over us.

Glen's eyes sparkled in the fading light. "You're figuring it out—aren't you!" he said softly. "You're figuring out how I did everything. And you understand—right? You understand why I had to pay those sisters back."

"Because of what Jackie did to you onstage in front of the whole school?" I asked. "Because of the Tarzan costume? Because none of them would stop teasing you about it?"

He nodded.

"But—but—what about your lawn mower?" I asked. "Your lawn mower went out of control and crashed. You almost cut off your foot."

Glen snickered. "Good one, huh? I faked that one. I wanted everyone to think you were responsible. I wanted everyone to think you were evil. Then I could get my revenge on those sisters—and everyone would blame you!"

He seemed so excited now, so pleased with himself. "You are so helpless, Maggie. You have no powers of any kind. But I can give you powers. I can share my powers with you. With just a touch."

He swiped his hand at me.

"No—!" I cried. "I don't want them! I don't want any powers, Glen. I just want—"

He didn't seem to hear my protests. "It's you and me now," he said, his eyes glowing in the shadowy light. "Just you and me against all of them."

He reached his hand out. "Come on. Share the power. Shake hands. Shake hands again, Maggie. It's you and me now. We'll show those sisters."

"No!" I cried again. "I—I won't!"

Eyes glowing wildly, he grabbed for my hand.

But I spun away from him. Stumbled over a fallen tree branch. Caught my balance and started to run.

"You can't run away from it!" he called after me.

And I gasped as I felt a force, a powerful force

holding me, pushing against me, holding me back.

"Nooooo!" I howled, and slammed my fists against the invisible wall in front of me. I dug my shoes into the dirt. I lowered my shoulder and pushed hard against the wall I couldn't see.

But he was holding me, using his strange power to hold me prisoner.

I ducked low. Tried to spin free.

But the invisible wall was all around.

"I warned you, Maggie!" he called. "You can't escape! You can't!"

And then dead leaves rushed up from the ground. Clumps of wet, dead leaves swooped up, swirled like a tornado— and swept over me. Weeds slapped at my face. Twigs and limbs snapped and swung at my waist, my legs.

"Stop!" I wailed. "Please—stop!"

The twigs, and weeds, and wet leaves stopped their wild whirl and sank around my shoes. And as they dropped back to the ground, I heard footsteps, hurrying toward us along the curving path.

Three grim-faced figures marching in a single row. The three Mullen sisters—swinging their fists as they walked. So angry. All three of them, so furious I could see it on their faces and in their stiff-legged, menacing steps.

I'm trapped, I realized.

Glen behind me, using his evil to hold me here in

place. And the sisters marching, advancing on me with such fury.

Trapped. Trapped . . .

What am I going to do?

I stared in horror at the sisters as they made their way toward us through the woods.

Jackie with her long hair flying behind her, beaded necklace bobbing up and down at her throat.

Judy, her clothes ripped and stained—but alive, alive!—marching in the middle, her eyes narrowed in anger.

Jilly, leaning on a crutch, struggling to keep up, her blond hair bouncing against her back, shaking her head, a scowl on her pale face.

They were my best friends, I thought bitterly. And now . . .

They think I am ruining their lives. All three of them—they believe I am trying to destroy them.

And so they are coming after me.

And in a few seconds . . . they will get me.

I took a deep breath and turned to Glen. "Okay!" I called in a whisper. I glanced over my shoulder, watching the sisters come closer.

"Okay, Glen. It's you and me," I whispered.

I reached out my hand to him. "I'll share the power. Let me have some of the power."

I could feel the invisible wall fade away. I took a step toward Glen. Then another. I could move again.

His eyes burned into mine. "You're serious? You'll help me destroy them for good?"

"Yes," I whispered, holding out my hand. "Yes. Hurry. I want the power again. They're almost here! Hurry!"

He stepped forward. Reached out to me. Grabbed my hand.

And squeezed it hard.

"Thank you!" I cried. "Yes! Thank you!"

"There they are!" Jackie cried, pointing.

"Maggie—" Jilly called, breathless from pulling herself through the woods with a crutch.

"Stay back!" I warned. I raised my hand, the hand Glen had just squeezed. "I'm warning you! Stay back!"

"This has to stop!" Judy shouted. "Those animals—they wanted to kill me!"

"Yes. This has to stop," Jackie repeated. "Now!"

I turned to Glen in time to see a cruel grin spread over his face. "The evil hasn't started yet!" he declared.

"It was Glen!" I cried, turning back to the sisters. "It was Glen the whole time! He has the powers! He—he was using me!"

"Yes!" Glen shouted, beaming with pride. "Yes, it was me all along! My power! My magic! But I made you believe your friend was evil. I made you believe!"

I saw the shock on the sisters' faces. But I didn't

wait for them to react. I knew I had to act quickly.

I spun around to face Glen. I raised my hand and waved it at him.

I concentrated all my thoughts . . . concentrated . . . concentrated . . . My arms tingled. Once again, my hands started to burn . . .

Glen opened his mouth in a cry of surprise. He was so stunned. He had no time to fight back.

And then he started to spin. Twirling like a top, he whirled around and around on one foot.

"Hey—!" He managed to call out. He tried to point at me. Tried to use his powers to stop me.

But I made him spin faster . . . faster. So fast he was sending up clouds of dirt and dead leaves.

"Thanks for sharing the power, Glen!" I shouted. "Thanks for sharing!"

And then I concentrated harder—and sent him flying off the ground. Higher . . . above the trees . . .

Spinning, his arms thrashing the air. Twirling faster and faster inside a cyclone of leaves, and twigs, and dirt.

And then I changed my thought. Concentrated . . .

I sent Glen crashing to the ground. He landed hard on his stomach. Let out a whoosh of air. Bounced once. Twice.

And before he could move, I changed my thought again. Pointed my finger down at him.

And watched his body shrink . . . shrink . . .

. . . Until he was a tiny, brown-and-white-striped chipmunk.

His tiny paws scrabbled over the dirt. He glanced up at me once with his round, black eyes. And then he scuttled around a fallen log and vanished under a blanket of dead leaves.

Finally I lowered my hand to my side. I started to breathe again.

Jackie rushed up to hug me. "You tricked him?"

I nodded.

"It's all over? The horror is over?" Judy asked. "It was Glen the whole time? Glen's evil powers?"

"Yes," I whispered. "He—he used me."

And then we were all hugging each other, all four of us at once. Hugging and laughing and crying all at the same time.

Finally, I let out a long sigh. "I can feel the power slipping away. I'm starting to feel normal."

"No—wait!" Jackie cried. "Before the power is gone for good—one favor!"

"Huh? What kind of favor?" I asked.

"Can you change our algebra grades?"

I laughed. Then I shut my eyes and concentrated . . . concentrated . . .

"Guess what?" I told them. "All four of us just made the Honor Roll!"

ABOUT THE AUTHOR

R.L. STINE says he has a great job. "My job is to give kids the CREEPS!" With his scary books, R.L. has terrified kids all over the world. He has sold over 300 million books, making him the best-selling children's author in history.

These days, R.L. is dishing out new frights in his series THE NIGHTMARE ROOM. When he isn't working, he likes to read old mysteries, watch *SpongeBob Squarepants* on TV, and take his dog, Nadine, for long walks around New York City, where he lives with his wife, Jane, and son, Matthew.

"I love taking my readers to scary places," R.L. says. "Do you know the scariest place of all? It's your MIND!"

Take a look at what's ahead in

THE NIGHTMARE ROOM #4
Liar Liar

As I fell back, I heard a high-pitched giggle in my ear.

I tumbled to the ground. Spun around quickly. Jumped to my feet.

And stared angrily at Jake.

"What are you doing out here?" I cried. My voice cracked.

That made Jake giggle even harder. His eyes flashed excitedly in the dim light. He loves scaring me. It's a total thrill for him to sneak up behind me and grab me or shout, "Boo!"

"What are you doing outside?" I repeated, grabbing him by the shoulders.

His grin grew wider. "I saw you coming."

I squeezed his tiny shoulders harder. "When did Mom get home? Does she know I went out?"

"Maybe," he replied. "Maybe I told her. Or maybe I didn't."

"Which is it?" I demanded.

"Maybe you have to find out," he said.

I loosened my grip. I smoothed the front of his T-shirt. "Listen, Jake—help me out here. I—"

The dining room window slid open. Mom poked her head out. "There you are, Rosssss."

I could tell by the way she hissed my name that she was totally angry.

"Get in here," she said. "Both of you. Right now." She slammed the window so hard, the glass panes shook.

She was waiting for us in the kitchen, hands pressed tightly against her waist. "Where were you, Rosssss?"

"Uh . . . nowhere," I said.

"You were nowhere?"

"Yeah," I said.

Jake laughed.

Mom's eyes burned into mine. "You weren't home when I got here. Were you?"

"Well . . . it's not what you're thinking," I said. "I mean, I didn't go to Max's party."

"Yes, you did!" Jake chimed in.

"Then where did you go?" Mom asked. "Why are you wearing a bathing suit? And why is it wet?"

"Uh . . . You see, Jake was watching a video. And I was so hot . . . I just went outside to cool off. I took a swim in our pool. Really. I knew I was grounded. So I just hung around the pool."

Jake laughed.

"Shut up, Jake!" I shouted. I spun away from him. "He just wants to get me in trouble, Mom. I was in the backyard. Really."

Mom scrunched up her face as she studied me. I could tell she was trying to decide whether or not to believe me.

The phone rang.

Mom punched the button on the speakerphone. "Hello?"

"Oh, hi. Mrs. Arthur?"

I recognized Max's voice. I could hear the party going on in the background.

"Yes, Max. Did you want to speak to Ross?"

"No," Max replied. "I was just calling to tell him he left his towel and his extra suit at my house."

I slumped onto a kitchen stool. Caught again.

Mom thanked Max and clicked off the speaker-phone. When she turned back to me, she did not have her friendly face on. In fact, she was bright red.

"I'm really worried about you, Ross," she said in a whisper.

"Huh? Worried?"

"I don't think you know how to tell the truth any-more."

"Sure, I do," I said. "I just—"

Mom shook her head. No. Really, Ross. I don't think you know the difference between the truth and a lie."

I jumped off the stool. "I can tell the truth!" I protested. "I swear I can. Sometimes I make up things because . . . because I don't want to get in trouble."

"Ross, I don't think you can stop making up things," Mom said softly. "When your father gets back from his shoot, we need to have a family meeting. We need to talk about this problem."

I stared at the floor. "Okay," I replied.

And then I suddenly remembered the boy in the pool. And I had to ask.

"Mom, can I ask you a strange question? Do I have a twin?"

She narrowed her eyes at me for a long moment. Then her answer totally shocked me. "Yes," she said. "Yes, you do."